Rowland Lyttleton Archer Davies

Poems and other Literary Remains

Rowland Lyttleton Archer Davies

Poems and other Literary Remains

ISBN/EAN: 9783337241933

Printed in Europe, USA, Canada, Australia, Japan

Cover: Foto ©Andreas Hilbeck / pixelio.de

More available books at **www.hansebooks.com**

POEMS

AND

OTHER LITERARY REMAINS

OF THE LATE

ROWLAND LYTTELTON ARCHER DAVIES,

OF TASMANIA.

Edited, with a Biographical Sketch,

BY CHARLES TOMLINSON, F.R.S.

LONDON:

EDWARD STANFORD, 55, CHARING CROSS, S.W.

HOBART, TASMANIA: J. WALSH & SONS.

MELBOURNE & SYDNEY: GEORGE ROBERTSON.

1884.

In Memoriam.

IF loving hands have often scattered o'er
    Thy grave, dear Rowland, brightest flowers of Spring,
    Summer and Autumn's blossoms scattering,
And verdant fronds from Winter's scantier store ;
A worthier tribute of thine own fresh lore,
    Hidden from sight till now, to light we bring,
    To show the world how deftly thou could'st sing
Of hills, woods, streams, glades, loves, unsung before.

If from thy home of homes, thy higher life,
    Thou still canst bless, thy blessing we would crave
    On this our pious work of charity :
These flowers of thought, with thy soul's fragrance rife,
    Wife, Mother, Friend now place upon thy grave,
    And dedicate to thy dear memory.

CONTENTS.

PAGE

THE POET ARTISAN	140
THE JOURNEY	147
DIVINATIONS	155
LOVE	157
SONG	159
DESPISE NOT	160
MAN	161
SEEMING	164
THE ENGINE-DRIVER	165
SORROW	168
THE WEDDING	169
CLIMBING THE MOUNTAIN	173
THE GAME OF CHESS	178
THE OLD YEAR	181
THE "PARKI"	183
IN A BOAT	186
SUMMER WINDS	188
A DREAM	190
THE RIVALS	193
YEARNINGS	196
NATURE'S INFLUENCES	198
DIRGE	200
THE STORM KING	202
DIRGE	204
SONG	205
LOST IN THE STORM	207
CHESS POEMS.—I. II. III. IV.	209

CHARADES.

UNFINISHED POEMS.

APPENDIX.

b

BIOGRAPHICAL SKETCH.

B

BIOGRAPHICAL SKETCH.

IF ever it should come to pass that the greatness of a nation is to be estimated not by its military and naval strength, its commerce, riches, and other exponents of material prosperity, but by its culture, and the general diffusion thereof among the masses of the people, then the men who have been most distinguished in literature, art, and science, will be regarded as that nation's true heroes. Our own country and many of the nations of Europe have long since sown the seed and reaped the harvests of intellectual life; but the fruit, unfortunately, is enjoyed by the comparatively few, while the masses still remain for the most part untouched by the refining and elevating influences of culture.

The United States of America have become alive to the necessity of securing a native literature; but our colonies are still in a backward condition as regards culture. The energies of a young colony are necessarily devoted to the securing of material comforts, in the direction of agriculture, trade, and commerce. That which at first was a necessity quickly grows into a habit, and habit soon becomes second nature. The useful arts supersede the fine arts, or, if the want of these should arise among the few, specimens of them are imported from older countries. It is the same with literature, and to a great extent with science. Their products can be imported, and are thus felt to be better than the results of native effort.

But should a distant colony really produce a man of literary genius, is it too much to suppose that the colonists would be proud of him, would cherish him, and never tire of admiring his work? And the more so, if that writer should identify himself with his native colonial life, manners, and scenery, and by his genius direct the attention of the world to a land whose beauties have been portrayed by his pen.

In many respects Rowland Lyttelton Archer Davies possessed these qualifications, as I shall endeavour to show in this memoir, and in the various specimens of poetry and prose which make up this volume. It must be remarked at starting that none of the papers here collected were ever intended for publication. Like many men of genius, Rowland threw off his verses in careless haste, as if to gratify some urgent mental instinct, and then became indifferent as to their future destiny. When he was sent to England for the completion of his education, he resided in my house as a pupil for the term of one year. My wife and I soon recognised his genius, and it was by her care that many of the poems were deciphered, copied, and thus preserved. During Rowland's residence in my house, my wife brought out a tale entitled " The Sisters " (published by the Christian Knowledge Society), in which she inserted a poem by Davies in two parts, in the first of which he described a Tasmanian forest in all its beauty, and in the second part the scene after the forest had been destroyed by fire. Some verses were also published at my request by the late Mortimer Collins, in a periodical that he was editing. With these exceptions, I am not aware that any of the matter contained in the following pages has appeared in print. After Rowland's death, his mother requested me to let her see anything of her son's that I happened to have by me, and accordingly I forwarded to her the collection that had been made by my late wife. Mrs. Davies consulted me how she could best leave some memorial behind her of the genius of her son, and I advised her to print a selection from his letters, prose sketches and poems, in a small volume to which I undertook to contribute a memoir of the author. Such is the history of the work which is now in the reader's hands.

Rowland L. A. Davies was born at the parsonage of Longford, in Tasmania, on the 28th of March, 1837. His father, the Venerable Rowland Robert Davies, was of a good old family of Mallow, county Cork. He was appointed Colonial Chaplain by the

Government of George IV., and after working with good effect in the colony during many years, he was invited in January 1853 by Bishop Nixon to fill the office of Archdeacon in the cathedral of Hobart. He died in 1880, in his 76th year, beloved and esteemed for his zealous and laborious work.

Rowland's early education was conducted at home, under the care of that best of all instructors, a good mother. While yet a child, he was passionately fond of music, and there was early developed in him a keen sense of the music of nature. When about four and a half years of age, as he was trotting on before his mother, the murmuring rippling sound of a brook caught his ear, and he stopped, saying: " Hush, mother ! What a beautiful voice !"

He also acquired early a taste for reading, which his father's well-stored library enabled him to gratify. He was especially interested in books of travel, which no doubt contributed to feed the restless wandering spirit which afterwards took possession of him. But the time had now arrived when this desultory method of gaining knowledge had to be exchanged for something like collegiate discipline. On the opening of the grammar school at Longford, by the Rev. D. Boyd, Rowland was entered as a day pupil. He soon became as distinguished as a scholar as he was beloved as a companion. However fond of intellectual work, he was ready for all kinds of exercise, games, and athletic sports with his schoolfellows. He also became a good and fearless rider. He had a spirited pony, on whose neck he would throw the rein, and gallop across the plain to school. He was also fond of wandering about the country, and on his half-holidays he would go about exploring, collecting fossils and plants.

A lady, in a letter to his mother, recalls him to mind thus :

" In the early days of our colonial life, when your beloved Rowley was a young, bright, handsome lad, full of enthusiasm for all that was noble and beautiful, never shall I forget his face in a drive from Launceston to Longford, whither you had kindly invited us, when he pointed out the Ben Lomond range and described to us the native flowers of Tasmania ; and I am sure that the fascination of his pleasant sunny smile, and genial kindly manner, must have been with him to the last, for such things have their root in a certain nobility of the soul, and can never pass away."

When the family left Longford, Rowland was entered at Christ's College, Bishopsbourne, where he so far distinguished himself as to gain the medal for Greek, and the prize for mathematics. He also continued to cultivate music ; he already played with the taste and feeling peculiarly his own, on the piano, and he now took lessons on the violin from one of the college tutors. His migratory life prevented him from keeping up his practice, and he afterwards became reluctant to play before an audience; but whenever he could be induced to take his place at the piano or the organ, his performances fell on the ear with an effect quite different to that of an ordinary touch. When alone of an evening, he said he never felt dull in the company of his books and his music, and after everyone had retired to rest except himself and his mother, he would often say to her, " Do you mind my going to the piano? I should like to strike a few soothing chords before I sleep." And he would go on extemporizing in the most charming manner in the dark room.

The love of books and of music, and frequent rambles among beautiful scenery, so far developed Rowland's character, that people who met him in the social circle of his father's house at St. David's or elsewhere, found him so well read, that they took him for a man of twenty-three or twenty-four, instead of a youth of seventeen.

While at college, Rowland wrote for the student's paper, *The Collegian*, the following *jeu d'esprit* :

" To the Editor of the *Collegian*.

Dear Sir,—In your paper of last Thursday week
A letter appeared, of which I must speak.
Its writer did in it mistakenly state,
That the mind of a man may be known by his gait.
The examples he gives may be true and correct,
But if for a while, Sir, the writer reflect,

He'll find many more which he never has named,
And which, if he had, he could ne'er have explained.
The way which I walk in, I now will relate ;
My character then, if he can, let him state.
My head I'm accustomed to raise very high,
And often my eyes are upturned to the sky ;
My countenance always demure and sedate,
The length of my back like a poker is straight ;
My arms swing about in a wonderful way,
They add to my beauty, my speed they delay.
I bear in my right hand a sasafras stick,
Which helps me on much when I want to go quick.
When I first 'gin to move, my legs give a jerk,
As if they would like all exertion to shirk ;
But once I can get my whole body in play,
My arms and my legs and my feet under weigh,
It would be a hard matter for me, Sir, to tell
How quickly I walk, or how far, and how well.
But here I must say that my legs are knock-kneed,
And that, of course, hinders a little my speed.
But still I ne'er walk e'en a little too slow,
And never walk fast excepting for show.
Thus always I go at a good steady pace,
Not limping with gout nor as running a race.
If my mind from all this he is able to tell,
His opinions henceforth I ne'er will repel.
I beg to subscribe myself, very dear Sir,
Your very obedient,

OLIVER PURR."

While at college, he also wrote to his mother the following remarks :

" I am reading a book by Mrs. Meredith, entitled ' My Home in Tasmania.' Considering that she is an English-woman, she certainly speaks pretty favourably of this country. She holds the same opinion as I do about the birds of Tasmania, and thinks that, far from being voiceless, they for the most part sing very beautifully. She likes however, the choir of magpies the best, which does not always suit the taste of strangers. For my part, I think that the wildest and most beautiful music I ever heard was the song of a chorus of magpies. Whenever I hear their voices they seem to send such a thrill through me. I have sometimes heard their singing in the stillness of the night, when I have been perhaps melancholy or sad, and their wild strains have seemed to harmonise with my thoughts; whilst at other times, when I have felt in a particularly joyous mood, their song has seemed to me merry and glad as my thoughts, as though they sympathised with my feelings and rejoiced because I rejoiced. But perhaps, after all, the singing of the magpie may not be really beautiful, but the reason for my being so fond thereof may be somewhat similar to the reason the Scotch are so fond of the harshest of all instruments—I mean, of course, the bagpipes."

The Archdeacon had a pretty retired house at Ferndene, on which he had bestowed much care in improving it, and surrounding it with trees and shrubs. It is situate at the foot of a hill, near to the mountain valleys and steep ridges, the former overlooking the city, the Derwent, with occasional peeps at the Channel, Storm Bay, and the ocean.

The time had now arrived when Rowland had to make choice of a profession. His mother naturally wished him to become a clergyman, but he said: " I could not be a clergyman, mother dear; I do not feel particularly called to the work, and everyone ought to be so, before taking those solemn vows; besides, there are so many requisites to make a really good and useful clergyman : talent, a good voice, earnestness, self-denial, devotion, and a winning manner. Oh ! I could not be a clergyman !" In fact, Rowland had to encounter those doubts and difficulties which more or less assail every earnest mind at some time or other, and often end in making their victim a nobler character than him who has never doubted at all ; or, as Thirlwall said of Arnold when at college, "Arnold's doubts are better than many men's beliefs." Rowland himself, in one of his letters, remarks,— "Most earnest men are tormented by doubts. Nay, as shadows show the sun, so doubts oftentimes give evidence of faith."

Rowland chose the profession of civil engineer, which I cannot help thinking was a mistake. His fitting vocation should have been literature. But so it was, that in 1854, on leaving college, he was placed in the office of Colonel Hamilton, R.E. Mr. Dawson, an architect, was the second in command, and had the chief superintendence of the new Government House then building. This was a great source of interest to Rowland, and gave him a taste for architecture. He remarked that it had given quite a new tone of thought and sight to him, for he looked at every building with a critical eye to its beauties or defects. After spending a year in this office, the

Archdeacon determined to send him to England in order to pursue his studies.

Before leaving his native land, Rowland's first professional work was to measure a space in the cathedral for a new organ, which had been ordered from England from the well-known maker, Bishop. When the instrument arrived, and its huge pipes were laid on the floor of the aisles, the organist was in great fear lest some portion should be too large for the building ; but his fears were groundless, for all the parts fitted exactly.

Before sailing, Rowland longed once more to visit the scenes he had so often explored amongst the hills, as had been his custom after office hours, returning home just at dark or by moonlight, laden with flowers, ferns, or fossils. On this occasion, intending to go further than usual, he chose a leisure afternoon, and his mother begged him to take with him a hatchet, for the purpose of marking the trees, so as to secure a safe retreat towards home ; since many persons had been lost in the thicket, during the mist or fog that sometimes comes on suddenly. A heavy thunderstorm overtook him as he was returning ; and feeling that there might be danger from the lightning, he threw away the hatchet. He sailed for England shortly after in the *Wellington*, when pacing the deck one day, some weeks after, he stopped abruptly at the sight of an object at his feet, and exclaimed, " That's my hatchet ! " " Your hatchet ? " said some

one, "How can that be yours?" "That's my hatchet!"
he repeated. "I threw it away on Mount Wellington."
On hearing this, the first mate came up, and said,
"Very likely, Mr. Davies; I went up the mount a few
days before we sailed, and I picked up that hatchet."

At the time when Rowland entered my house, I
had a number of other pupils, who had attained some
distinction as prizemen at King's College. Rowland's
modest bearing, good temper, and undoubted ability,
soon secured for him that respect which the others
were not at first disposed to yield to colonial training.
The young men were full of life and activity, and
were interested in most of the topics of the day;
talked much of authors, new books, pictures, music,
&c., as well of the studies in which they were engaged,
and were not slow in criticising their professors
and fellow-pupils at college. When thus engaged,
Rowland's merry twinkling eye would often lead the
disputants to appeal to him, and his judgment, marked
as it was with a keen appreciation of character and
extensive knowledge of books, English and classic,
soon came to be received with respect. On one
occasion we had been discussing the merits of
English hexameters, as exemplified by Longfellow
and others, when one evening one of my pupils,
whom we will name Little, had on this and other
occasions shown a disposition to be bumptious, and
to apply the word "stupid" to what he called the

" young gentlemen at college." One of those present, taking it personally, gave the speaker a rap on the head, and on my going into the study to resume work, having heard of the circumstance, I admonished the victim in a hexameter line :

" Never, O Little, again, wilt thou call the young gentleman stupid."

to the great amusement of them all.

Rowland was very fond of goodnatured banter, which admirably served the purpose of the moment, but cannot be easily illustrated by example. I remember, however, on one occasion, a lady asked him somewhat solemnly, " How did you employ your time during your long voyage to England?" " Oh," said Rowland, " I lay on my back on the deck, looked up into the sky, and smoked." " That is not the way," said the lady severely, " in which an intelligent young man should spend his time!" " But I am not an intelligent young man," responded Rowland. The fact really was that he was the life of the ship, and published a manuscript journal twice a week, giving the real or supposed life of that little floating world.

Rowland was omnivorous in his reading. Some one lent him the early volumes of ' Blackwood,' and he gloated over the savage criticisms which were then in fashion. Most of the literature in my library that he was not already acquainted with, occupied much of his time. Indeed, his taste was so decidedly literary, that I could not refrain from secretly lamenting the choice he had made of a profession. His heart was not in his work ; he pursued it in a desultory kind of manner, and although he afterwards laboured at it with more effect, it was rather for conscience' sake than for love. During our many pleasant walks and talks, literature was the subject of our discussions, and poetry above all was his favourite theme. My wife, as already noticed, encouraged this taste, and got him to open up his stores of literary compositions, which he held in careless confusion, and were all but unintelligible—so bad was the writing—and persuaded him to write more. It is to be lamented, that what Pope says of Dryden—

> " E'en copious Dryden wanted, or forgot,
> That last and greatest art, the art to blot,"

applied in full force to Rowland. He could not be brought to revise his work ; to polish it so as to give clearness, method, and point to it. As it was produced, so it was left : the inspiration of the moment was all-sufficient for him, and the *labor limæ* was intolerable. Hence the poems that are collected in this little volume, full of beauties as they are, have defects in the way of form, and the thought is some-times obscure and badly worked out ; but I have not deemed it right to work much at them in order to make them more perfect, feeling that they represent the author's mind better in their present form, than if polished by another hand, unguided by the author's inspiration. Still, I have done something ; for in many cases the lines were too rough and unfinished to be presentable. I have removed some discords in the rhythm of the verse, and have supplied many blanks which were left by the copyists of the later poems (the MS. of which still remains in Tasmania), from sheer inability to make out the writing, or from portions being torn, or from the MS. being worn almost to shreds in the author's pocket. Many of the poems had no titles to them, and these I have supplied. Hence, the labour of revision has been considerable, and I have devoted a good deal of time to it from love to the memory of the author, as well as to that of my dear wife, who prized Rowland's friendship and genius so highly.

But it is time now to let Rowland give his own impressions of England, as expressed in extracts from the letters that he sent home. It should be remarked that, in his own country, the trees retain their foliage all the year round, and during his first year's residence in England, he was particularly struck with the fall of the leaf, the autumnal tints, and the bare skeletons of the trees in winter. Most of the following extracts are from letters addressed to his mother, and are sufficiently intelligible to be given without further comment, except to remark on the absence of dates in the extracts, for they are for the most part absent in the original letters :

"You cannot think how fortunate and happy I am in being in the house of Mr. and Mrs. Tomlinson. I like them much, and I think they like me *tolerably*. Here I have slipt into the society of professors of science, and of eminent poets and literary men : an immense advantage to me. You tell me always to give you the dark as well as the bright side of the picture. I have, thank heaven, no dark side to give you just now."

_____

" The six or seven Tasmanians that are studying here are, I think, getting on well. They will be for the most part strong, earnest men, with perfect straightforwardness and rectitude. And now I, amongst the number, try my best to do my duty, with many shortcomings, though less frequent perhaps than formerly, but still with many. I am gaining, I think, the victory over self, with whom my greatest battling has been ; and now I strive to have better and higher aims than formerly, more without the circle of self, remembering that all true heroism is unselfishness. and that self-sacrifice is the very keystone of Christianity. The very young man is by force an egotist ; he has so much to do with the struggles within himself, half smothered, perhaps, at the very commencement of his pilgrimage in the slough of despair, that he has no time to look around and see how many others about him are all striving with the self-same hopes and doubt. A man must set himself aside before he can be truly happy ; he must learn his true place in the world, and that is not easy. It is long before he can say with St. Paul, ' I would gladly be accursed for Christ's sake, if by that means I might save some.' However, perhaps after all I am but the bond-slave of self."

_____

C

" All life then is an actual prayer,
And most unregarded things,
So they be of faith and love,
Bear us, as on angel's wings,
To the throne of God above ;
For a life of love is God's own prayer."

———

" 1856.
" You think I should be disappointed in Tasmania on
seeing it again. I think not. However, it is not only a
remembrance of its beauty makes me desire to return to
it ; for I have now come to consider that beauty dwells not
alone in any particular place, but everywhere, had we only
the eyes to see it. Beauty is from within, not from without. But, as I was saying, it is not the beauty alone
which makes me look forward to Tasmania, but a sort of
idea that I was not born there for no purpose, but that
whatever my mission is, good or bad, small or great, it
lies there. Not without meaning are those impulses im-
planted in us which lead us ever on to our birth-place as a
final resting place. Is it not an unconscious recognition
of the fact, that we have there a something to perform?
But after all this may be a mere brain idea, one of those
thought-bubbles that float now and then through the
brain, shortly to vanish in ' thin air.'"

———

" There is a great deal of beauty in English scenery, in
its green lanes and hedgerows, and old ivy-covered
churches, and its leafless trees have a peculiar but infinite
beauty ; they are exquisite against a clear sky, though in
dull weather I cannot find much to say of them."

———

" Spring, 1856.
" The dreary winter, with its thick fogs, its soaking,
drizzling rains, and its cold east winds, is almost over, and
the blessed spring is waking the whole country into new
life and beauty. Even London (a pleasant place withal)

has lost its smoke-dried appearance, for the trees and
hedges in the parks and squares are fringed with the
delicate green of the first bursting leaves. From many
of the dusky windows kindly-faced primroses and geraniums peep out at one with their pleasant, country-like
glances. Women carry about in the streets large baskets
of homely, sweet-smelling wallflowers, while the donkey-
carts, with piles of rhubarb and cauliflowers, have great
bunches of daffodils and other beautiful flowers, such as
we should despise, perhaps, but such as are precious here.
With the spring of all the bright leaves and flowers old
fancies seem to spring anew, old thoughts to break again
into blossom, and I have strange longings too, half pleasant and half sad : longings to see the dear old country,
with its mighty trees, its blue mountains and gushing
rivers ; still stronger longings for the 'tender grace' of
dear familiar faces ; and, strongest of all, the most pleasant,
the most joyous, and yet most sad. are the longings I feel
to be with you, to hear you, to see you, and to talk with
you. I often do all this in imagination. Just as the
candles are lighted I pop in, rush downstairs to ask if we
can have an early tea, come up four steps at a time, have
a game of romps with the children, then into the dining-
room. where I sit down and begin a quiet chat with you."

"MANCHESTER, *Sept.* 15, 1857.

" MY DEAREST MOTHER,

" Here begins my threatened journal. This is a strange,
whirling, bustling life, that people lead here, and my
business for this time is whirling enough too, whizzing
away on the engine from place to place ; but in the evening, when work is over, and I have had tea, I sit myself
down at the open window, put the lamp out, and spend
hours in watching the stars, or the town, with its glimmering lamps, andthe occasional scenes in the streets. I
feel so calm and quiet after those hours, and I think of all
sorts of calm, and quiet, and pleasant things. I think

much of you and home, and of getting back again, and of how I should like to drop in 'unbeknown,' and see if you would know me. I think you would, notwithstanding all the alterations, real or supposed. Now that I am in Manchester, I must tell you something about it. It is an enormous city, even after London. You may wander on for miles in every direction, and still no country ; nothing but whirling mills, warehouses, factories, and dingy streets without end ; or if by chance you do smell a green field or two, a little further on you are again in another apparently endless town ; for in fact a great many towns, such as Oldham, Stockport, Ashton, &c., are in reality merely suburbs of Manchester. At present the place is filled with visitors at the principal hotels, on account of the Exhibition of Art Treasures. . . . When one gets a little way out of Manchester, and looks down on the town, the scene is indeed a strange one, but with a beauty of its own. It seems one gigantic smoke-monster—a dream of smoke, as it were, with spires, and chimneys tall and tapering, appearing confusedly through the mist. There is a mystery about the whole which strikes one very much. The knowledge, too, of the energy and force concealed under all that dense mass of vapour, adds somewhat to the effect of the scene. A grand city has somehow to me something of the power, and calls up some such feelings as the perfect grandeur and solitude of a mountain. I always, when I get back to London, feel that strange wild joy that I used to feel on Mount Wellington. I am lonely at Manchester, having no one to speak to. I have had no books either, so have had to amuse myself with the night scenes around me and my own thoughts. The former is a fruitful source of amusement, as it is indeed anywhere and everywhere. I could not desire a more admirable diversion for an hour, than standing against a lamp-post in some of the principal thoroughfares of London, and watching all that goes on, and everybody that passes by : there is study enough for the physiognomist, the moraliser, or the satirist. I think a thoughtful man ought never to be tired of London, except, of course, when a memory of green fields comes over him, and he wants a little country air, and so on. Besides, a total change of that sort is needed now and then. Most London, or sedentary London at all events, finds its way into a green field, or wanders between two hedges, on a Sunday. It is delightful to see people enjoying themselves on the Sabbath excursions, which are so arranged by the railway company in the summer months, as to be within the reach of most of the most beautiful and interesting places in England. They come back tired, hungry, sleepy, and delighted, better, body and soul, for their pleasure, and ready for all the toils of the week. The fresh clear air, the beautiful earth, with God's blue sky bending over everything, does these smoke-smothered dwellers in the town more good than any sermons or service whatever. Truly, the 'Sabbath was made for man.' The strict Sabbatarian doctrine is, or would be, very injurious in a place like London, morally, physically, and intellectually ; that is, the idea of worshipping God more on one day than another—being more religious on Sunday. To the religious man all times and seasons are alike fitted for the worship of God. Nay, the truly religious man *never* ceases to worship God ; but, as St. Paul says, ' whether we eat or drink, or whatever we do, do all to the glory of God.' The Christian and the philosopher, and any practical thinker, knows that eternity is dedicated to God, so that the worship of the Eternal Being must be eternal, constant ; not spasmodic, as Sunday worship often is. To the great majority of Londoners Sunday is the only day for healthy exercise, country air, and good, wholesome out-of-door amusements ; thus, debarring them from any of these things is injurious.

"There is a very good library in Manchester ; it is about the only perfectly free library I know, of any value, except the S. Geneviève at Paris. The British Museum

Library is free to you, if you get recommended by persons of known respectability; but here a perfect stranger in the poorest rags may walk in and be supplied with any books the library contains. I was reading there to-day ; it is a beautiful and lofty room, every convenience, arm-chairs, matting on the floor to prevent disturbing noises, pens, ink ; and I was reading Mrs. Gaskell's life of Charlotte Brontë, an admirable biography of a most rare and extra-ordinary woman, by also a most rare woman, Mrs. Gaskell herself being the author of some of the best novels of the day. Charlotte Brontë, you know, was the celebrated 'Currer Bell,' who wrote that wonderful book, 'Jane Eyre.' I would advise you to read her life.

"My journal has come to an untimely end, for I had about ten days ago to run up to London, and have only just got back, owing to various things, and find the mail goes to-night."

"MANCHESTER, *November*.

"DEAREST MOTHER,

"Again my journal is once more about to begin: my work here is of such a sort that, though for the most part I have little to do, still I am obliged to be about, for fear of there being something to attend to. This is very unpleasant. During the spare time I might have walked about Lancashire and Yorkshire with great ease, and much pleasure and profit. As it is I have only managed to snatch one or two single days, enough to please and tantalise, but that is all. On Wednesday I had a delight-ful walk. I started from a little town called Colne, in Lancashire, where I had stayed before ; there are some quaint old houses there, and an interesting old church, with a sun-dial over the porch, placed very strangely, some-thing like a pepper-box : my rude sketch from memory is something like the position, the square thing at the top being the dial. Well, when I left Colne, the road was almost all up-hill till I came to a little toll gate ; here the roads divided, and I was in great doubt which to take, so walked back again till I met a man who told me. The weather, which had been fine at starting, began to grow over-cast, cloud after cloud came drifting over the moors, and I was soon in a thick, soaking Scotch mist. I was very sorry for this, for I was walking along the ridge of the hills, and the ground falling at either side of me, I should have had magnificent views up the various valleys, Now and then the mist would rise a little, and I could see trees, fields, houses, &c., dim and shadowy in the green valleys below me. The moors were or seemed extremely lonely, not a sound but the patter of my own feet, and the occasional barking cry of the grouse ; there seemed to be nothing moving, not a breath of air, nothing but the white crawling mist wrapping up the hills slowly and silently. After a time it became very pleasant, the mist clearing off and the scenery being most beautiful. Besides I saw ' Bolton Abbey ' in Yorkshire, one of the most beautiful places in its way I ever beheld. The woods too, which are there very fine, were in all the glory of autumnal tints, every shade of red and yellow spangling the green, I came back to Colne in the evening, where I had a long argument with an old magistrate about phrenology and Greek, and learnt that I had missed seeing some of the places about Bolton best worth seeing ; as one always finds. for what one does not see is sure to be better than all else. It was not a very adventurous walk, though I have since had some that really were. I have been hurried about the last week or two, and have just returned from Manchester to London.

"I was delighted to get back to London ; it seems such a jolly, kind-hearted, over-grown polypus of a place. When I got out at King's Cross and about there, I felt quite happy. I knew all the long streets, all the drivers and 'bus men, and it seemed, everybody. London is the only place in England that I really like.

"At Easter I had a few days' holiday, and went down

to ——, and spent a day with a wise old man, who lives like a hermit there in an old ruined house. He says Dr. —— (a celebrated physician in London) and myself are the only two people out of his own village who know his address. I thought of writing an account of my visit and adventures for your edification, and calling it the 'Ruins of Palmyra,' the name he gives his house. If you have ever read the Hyperion of Longfellow, the Berkeley in the story is the same man—many years younger, of course. He is the only man I ever knew who said he was perfectly happy, and I thoroughly believe that he is."

———

"Yesterday I heard the most beautiful sermon I ever heard in my life from Kingsley. I felt as if I could have gone to him like a little child, that he might put his hand upon me and bless me."

———

" Manchester is a strange and wonderful place, but I am very tired of it now. One day I got a walk in the country on the Lancashire and Yorkshire moors. Amongst other places I saw 'Haworth,' now rather famous as the residence of the three Miss Brontë's, who wrote under the names of Currer, Ellis, and Acton Bell. Currer (Charlotte Brontë), the authoress of 'Jane Eyre,' 'Shirley,' 'Vilette,' &c., is the most celebrated. Her life, which was published a short time ago, is already in a third edition. Haworth has become quite a shrine for literary pilgrims. You should read the life and some of her works to act as a commentary. Haworth is a little town, situated in a wild country. I enjoyed my walk over the moors very much. I passed a very pretty little hamlet called 'Whycolor,' or some such name—I spell from sound, never having seen the word written. There was a ruined hall there, of which a Yorkshire woman told me a strange story of a squire of the name of ——, who lived there, and was greatly addicted to cock-fighting. When he was on his death-bed, and too ill to see them, he had a mirror opposite to him, so contrived that while they were fighting on the lawn he could see them reflected in the glass without stirring. He died, they say, while watching them. A strange fancy, was it not? People say the old hall, or one particular room in it, is haunted."

———

" I was at Lichfield Cathedral yesterday. It certainly is very beautiful ; there is a certain glory about these old buildings that everybody must feel, partly from their own intrinsic grandeur, and partly also from the numberless associations connected with every stone. They have an indefinable strong power over me, filling me with memories of a strange past, till those times seem to come again. The present passes away from my thoughts, till all things are wrapt in a mist of past thoughts and past emotions, till I myself seem to belong to the olden ages. I went also to St. Chad's, which is a curious picturesque old place. Gresley is rector there. You recollect his ' Siege of Lichfield,' a pleasant book, but making, as I think, the worse appear the better cause. He is a very kind, good old man, I believe, and the church is a pretty old place. I like the old churches and places in England, and I love the past which they recall, though I hold the present to be the better, and the future better still. As Tennyson says—

' For I doubt not through the ages one increasing purpose runs,
And the thoughts of men are widened with the progress of the suns.'

" I am now in the iron counties, near what is called the Black Country. I am staying with Mr. Bolton for a fortnight. They are very kind to me, as indeed every one is, and people I know always seem glad to see me ; indeed, I don't see well how people could be much kinder or more hospitable than they are in England, though some of them hedge and ditch themselves round with ceremony ; but once get within the lines and they are very different, for 'All things are less dreadful than they seem.'

" I am combining pleasure and profit : one day going over ironworks, and on another, over old places and churches, though the pleasant part, by the way, helps me on with my architecture.

" In your last letter you talk much of coming to England for good, but very kindly say that wherever I am to live you also will live. Of course it must be the other way : wheresoever you and my dear father choose, I will choose ; but I would venture to advise you well to consider it. It is a great thing to have a place that has been a home for years and years : to have the scene of one's labours, the scene of one's joys and sorrows, of pleasures and trials—I say trials and sorrows, for to me they hallow places almost more than our pleasures. They are bitter, truly, in the tasting, but oftentimes passing sweet in the remembrance. It will be a sad thing too, I take it, to leave all old places we have loved for mere beauty. It will be sad, I say, to leave them even though there were nothing beyond their beauty, but there is much. Think what it would be to leave for ever all those blue mountains we love so well ! Will you not long for them here in England, as you look from your window and see a 'beautiful home view' as they call it, with a green field and a hedge, or a 'fine wild extensive view,' just a common, or a heathery moor or down ? You forget the climate, too."

———

" 1857.—I have left Mr. Simpson's works, and now am learning surveying in the offices of Saunders and Mitchell. I am to be with them six months, and expect at the end of that time, if all goes well, to be initiated into the mysteries of field work. I heard one of the street bands this evening singing that pretty melody, 'Old Folks at Home.' You can't think how it made me long to be with you again. I would give anything, too, for a glimpse of those great blue mountains, and a plunge into one of those delicious basins in our beautiful mountain streams. There is nothing in England south of the Lakes to be compared with them. The rivers are few, sluggish, and of a nasty brown mud colour, but the skies and the sun are the chief want here; the remembrance makes the dulness of the English atmosphere more obtrusive. From November to May the skies seem to have a perpetual headache, whether from weeping so much, or what, I cannot say."

"BROUGHTON IN FURNESS, LANCASHIRE.

"Mr. Saunders has brought me up here surveying (under another besides himself), on a proposed line of rail from the above place to Coniston Head. You have heard of the lake, and can guess in what a beautiful country I am situated. I can scarcely believe I am in England, for at every turn I find some resemblance or fancied resemblance to scenes in Tasmania. I have made rather an advance in the world, as all my expenses are paid as long as I am at this place surveying.

"Yesterday we had not much to do, and so I took a long walk over the moors and mountains with the assistant surveyor, under whom I have been working the last few days. He was regularly beaten before he got home, and had to lean on my shoulder. We saw a beautiful waterfall, or rather series of waterfalls, a 'tarn' or two, and some very picturesque mountain ranges. We came to a strange little country inn after our long walk, and not before we were very hungry and somewhat wet, as we had to cross the 'Esk' in a very primitive bush-like fashion. After having something to eat at the inn, I left my companion by the fire, and climbed up a hill to see a number of Druid stones arranged in strange figures, chiefly of a circular or elliptical form. When I came back to the inn, I found 'the other young man' had gone on more than half an hour before, and as it was getting dark and the way somewhat uncertain, I set out at a pretty good pace, and succeeded, in about six miles or so, in overtaking my friend, who was rather astonished, as he walked at what he called a furious rate. Coming over the moor and along the hill side by moonlight, was very enjoyable. It was a wild, gusty, changeable night, the moon coming out every now and then by fits and starts, and lighting up the path, glittering as it was with showers, and seemed far ahead, winding like a great snake in amongst the dark heathery moor.

" Broughton, where we are at present staying, is close to the river Duddon ; on and about here Wordsworth wrote a volume of sonnets, so the ground is to some extent classical.

" Furness Abbey is not very far from here, and I saw it for a few minutes as the train stopped close to it, and there was a slight delay. It was wonderfully beautiful, the only ruin I have yet seen beautiful for its own sake alone. I will not attempt to describe it ; suffice it, for your imagination, to conjure up a secluded 'gully,' fringed with moss-begrown trees ; at the green bottom of the said gully, tall arches perfect and imperfect ; shattered door-ways and broken pillars, a plentiful sprinkling of ivy and divers creeping plants, hundreds of rooks cawing amid the arches, and no end of associations ; with these materials your fancy can easily (aided by remembrance), form a picture not very unlike the reality. The church here is not very striking ; however there is, where you would probably expect anything but it, a curious old Norman door ; it is likely the present church was built on the site of some ruined Norman building, and the door of the old church, being firm, was built into the old superstructure. It is not the only instance I know of the door being 'old Norman,' whereas the rest of the church was compara-tively modern. The people here are very primitive and proportionably stupid, very different to Londoners. I quite look forward to going back to London, to speaking

to anybody and everybody, and finding they can all understand you. My companion, who is like myself a kind of
adopted cockney, amused me by comparing the roar of a
cataract to the rumble of a brewer's cart."

"The Temple, Westminster Abbey, and St. Stephen's,
Walbrook, are my favourite churches. Dr. Croly preaches
at the latter ; he is well worth hearing and seeing, though
I think I like the Bishop of Oxford's sermons better than
any I have ever heard. Were you ever at the Temple
Church ? It is, I think, the most beautiful in London.
The oldest church is St. Bartholomew's, Smithfield. It is
old Norman work, begun in Henry I.'s reign, by an old
monk of the name of ' Rahere.' As Smithfield was at
that time a mere morass, the building of the church was
looked upon as a miracle. Some of the work would be
very beautiful, only it has been ' beautified and restored '
by some idiot, whitewashed and made hideous, all the
defects and gaps in the carvings worn by the hand of time
appearing, in consequence of the whitewash, like bad new
work.

"I enjoy a ramble in old London very much ; not a
corner but is stuck full of associations and recollections.
New London is dull in the extreme."

"I wonder how you all are now. I quite pant to be with
you all again, and to see that intense blue sky of ours, for
there is nothing like it here. For the most part the sky
is dull and leaden, and when it is blue you can only just
look at it as a blue surface, as it were. But we look into
ours higher and higher, and higher still, yet never seem
to reach the end of it. It is an incalculable blessing to
have such a sky continually over one's head—to have
such a climate so buoyant and exhilarating. I would
give anything to be in it for a day or two ; to live
once again, to feel the full bliss of existence. Here,

though I am very well, I am not conscious of life—never experience the grand pleasure, the joy of mere living. I may be in an unquiet sleep, for all I know to the contrary; but in Tasmania I knew that I lived, I felt life in every breath : here I may be in a dream—it may be all a dream, this England, at least my being here. This may be a dream letter ; I may after all be asleep in the attic in St. David's Parsonage, and may wake just in time to hear the clock strike eight, and find myself too late for church. There is a great deal though in this England which is wonderfully pleasant and instructive, in London especially. There are the thousands and thousands of people coming and going in the streets—this is the grandest sight of all. Then there are the picture galleries, the facilities for hearing, seeing, doing, and learning : things which we cannot have in Tasmania. Then in the country there is an endless beauty of garden and greenland, with their hedgerows and close avenues of trees ; then there are the quiet villages, with their old-fashioned taverns and ivied churches, filled as they are with strange remembrances and old romances. There is an infinite beauty in the old mouldering, time-worn buildings, and their associations and strange stories ; but one look at one of our mountains and at our bright blue skies and clear buoyant sunshine is worth a world of this mouldering, decrepit old age. And so, with a sigh for Tasmania and all of you, I will conclude this letter, whose happy fate of soon seeing you all, and tasting that blessed air, you may be sure I envy."

" I have made acquaintances now in almost every class of society. I should think I know some hundreds of people of one sort and another ; and I think there is some good to be found in all, if you will but look. I have scarcely ever met a person in my life from whom I could not learn something. I have had good lessons taught me by an old beggar woman ; and about these poor old beggars, many good people, when they visit them, go as if doing a kindness, when in all probability they do themselves a far greater kindness and more good than they can possibly do the old women. I think that the poorest and most unregarded people, if they strive to do their duty, should be seen to and visited by the greatest, humbly and reverently, as unto sons and daughters of God—which Christ teaches us they are. I am inclined to think that God takes more especial care of those whom men despise —the poor in intellect and so forth—just as the mother takes often more loving care of a deformed child."

"MY DEAREST MOTHER,

"I have been in a great hurry-skurry lately, else I should have written a longer letter than this is going to be. I have been changing my habitation, and am now ensconced in new quarters. I only entered them this evening. I have changed my work also, and am now in a locomotive engine shop at Bow, one of the eastern suburbs of London. The work is admirably fitted to correct my bad habits. since I have to be at work at 6 A.M., only five minutes' grace being allowed; so I have to be up early, punctuality being absolutely necessary. In the evening I have plenty of time to myself. I quite rejoice in returning to manual labour again, after so long an interval. It does indeed make me enjoy the evenings. A day spent in bodily labour makes a musty old tome in the evening a perfect paradise. Body and soul thereby are kept as it were in perfect tune : they no longer clog each other, but are as one. Labour of the body alone, or of the mind alone, is alike injurious. Here we have in England the heavy sheepish faces of the country boor on the one hand, and the white unmanly face and form of the London clerk, or the profound book-worker. The old Greeks knew this well; they knew that strength of thought could not be obtained unless the body was kept in a perfect system of exercise. So the students of Plato, whose minds were of the strongest, obtained that strength in a great measure by the severity of their corporal discipline. I daresay, too, you may have remarked the effect of labour on the minds of the first founders of Christianity. There is no need for St. Paul to tell us he worked with his own hands : we see it in every sentence, we feel it in every word. More and more I see the necessity of bodily labour. More and more I am struck with the complicated evils, moral and physical, that result from its absence."

———

"DEAR MRS. ———

"I promised to go to ——— on Saturday, that is to say to-day, and I have promised to go to 'Stoke Pogis' on Sunday week; so you must let me make a Sabbath of some week-day when I can leave my work tolerably early, and you will preach a better sermon to me than any gentle curate can do, and sing besides some of your sweet Sabbath songs that do so strangely haunt me. I should like to learn the secret of that peculiar power your voice possesses, it is something very much deeper than mere sound. I have heard, or rather felt the same mystery when, after a storm, the sea swells on a level shore ; once or twice I have felt it in forests ; but never in the song of birds, nor yet in the cadences of voices. I listen and wonder. I should have answered your very kind note or notelet (what is the diminutive of note?) before this, only I intended to have walked down to Harrow this morning before breakfast ; for I get up now at daybreak, or thereabouts, because I consider such early rising to be one step, though a very small one, towards the pure and right life which I do one day hope to live. In working out our salvation, body must have a voice; soul must not have it all her own way. I look upon body as a sacred trust, and he who has learnt a true reverence therefor is not 'far from the kingdom of God.' Your friendship has been a great blessing to me. I am always better after being with you, much more humble, trustful, and childlike. You don't believe in my being childlike ; but I really am much more so

now than I ever was before. I never had any child-
hood ; as a compensation, I hope to have the child heart
now. Tell —— that I have read very attentively the
later numbers of the *Normandy Chronicle*. In them I
find much pleasant wit and genial writing, but much also
of the most feminine bad grammar—relative, without
anything to relate to. It is all owing to the natural secre-
tiveness of women's nature ; for women are essentially hiding or concealing animals. You love secrets
and mysteries intensely, and that is why you can't keep
them."

Rowland arrived in his native land on April 2nd,
1859. He appeared to his friends bright and content,
yet thoughtful, for beneath his cheerfulness was an
anxiety to procure employment. He had hoped to
be engaged on the waterworks that were about to
be constructed ; but some of the elder members
of the town council feared that he might be too
young for such an appointment, and consequently
procured an engineer from Melbourne. He was the
more disappointed, as his duties would frequently
have taken him to his favourite mountain, the streams
of which were to be concentrated for the city supply.
Accordingly he proceeded to Victoria, where he
succeeded in gaining an appointment on a railway,
which he held for a short time, and then returned to
take charge of a mine at Clunes which turned out to be
a more important and lucrative post. While manager
there, he was injured in a railway accident at Richmond,
which threw a shadow over the remainder of his life.

D

It appears that the line was unfinished, although it was occasionally used. The stone ballasting was lying in heaps between the rails, ready for spreading. Rowland had been absent for a few days for his Christmas holidays, during which he paid a visit to Melbourne, to see a fellow passenger from England, who was living at Richmond. They sat up till a late hour, talking about books and poetry, and although it was a stormy night, blowing and raining hard, Rowland would not stay till the morning, but determined to return to the city by rail, knowing that he would be in time to catch the last train; so he ran down the bank or cutting of the new line to Cremorne, which had lately been opened, when he heard, amidst the din of the storm, the noise of the train proceeding, as he supposed, up to Richmond. But unfortunately it was coming up behind him, and struck him down. The train was passing round a sharp curve from Cremorne, approaching a terminus, so that the speed was slackened, and the lamps enabled the engine driver to see an object on the line. He was found on one side of the rail between two heaps of ballast, in a pool of blood, from some terrible wounds in the head. He was conveyed to his uncle's house at Geelong, where he was attended by Dr. Day. Rowland's first anxiety was that no account of the accident should be published in the Melbourne papers, and he sent a friend to the different offices, begging them to omit all mention of the accident, lest his parents should be alarmed at reading the account. He then got some one to hold a book before him while he wrote home with his own hand, requesting his mother to come to him. His parents started by the first steamer, and in answer to their anxious inquiries the doctor told them that two great dangers were to be feared : one was that erysipelas might set in, which the great heat was likely to favour (the Christmas in those parts being the height of summer) ; the second danger was that inflammation of the membranes covering the brain might come on. But the healthy life that Rowland had led made him escape both these dangers, so that at the end of three weeks, his parents accompanied him to Clunes, where he resumed his duties, the doctor thinking it better for him to go to his post, than to fret at a distance. After remaining a day or two with him, his parents left Rowland, his head still bound up, in the charge of kind friends who had long known and appreciated him, and under their care he gradually recovered some measure of health and strength.

Soon after resuming his duties, the directors resolved to discontinue working the mine for some time, and Rowland had again to seek employment. His love of adventure tempted him to join a Government exploring party in Victoria. He seems to have recovered his health and spirits in a remarkable degree, for in a letter to his mother, dated from near Navarre, he says :

" I cannot easily help being well, with the sort of life we lead here. Up at six, a plunge into the water-hole, break-fast, fresh air, and work till tea again, and bed about ten. I have not had a cold for I don't know how long—not, I think, since I first went to Gundoit, and have been leading the life you feared so much. I am glad you like the 'Summer Winds.' You may take it as a rule in my effusions, that when I am the first person singular, the thoughts and utterances are not supposed to be mine, but some imaginary character, good or bad, as the case may be."

The following extracts will also show the kind of life led by him about this time :

" I enclose a few verses on a bit of dirty paper. I meant to have copied and corrected them, but have not time just now. Of course they have nothing to do with me now ; they might have been true to a certain extent some six years ago, when I used to lead a dreamy life. I mean them to be thoughts of a dreamy, speculative, studious, unpractical sort of man, who begins to find out there is something in the world besides mere know-ledge.

" I send them because you said you would like them sent you now and again. Most of my effusions are rather too fierce and satirical to suit you, but these are quiet enough. They came into my head on Sunday, as I lay basking in the sun, watching the wind playing in the gum leaves.

" You ask about our prospects here in the bush. First and foremost, there is a large reward for the discovery of a gold field ; secondly, the prospecters get a large

claim or grant of land—in fact, if we do find a payable
gold field we have our fortunes well begun, if not made.
As yet we are only partially successful ; that is to say,
have found just enough gold to show there is more
somewhere. We can scarcely expect greater success in
so short a time. For the rest, I am learning a good deal
and gaining practical experience in mining and gold
deposits generally. I seem to be perfectly well, only
a little short-winded to what I used to be before my
accident. Fresh air, regular hours, and simple food do a
man no harm for a few months. We amuse ourselves in
the evenings pretty well ; they got me on the phreno-
logical tack the other night, and I had a great feeling of
bumps, and told their characters nearly all round, apparently with some truth. We are talking of choosing
some man's life, and for one to give a sort of lecture on it,
and for the rest to have a discussion afterwards, on
Saturday nights, as we sit up later on that night than at
ordinary times."

" October 14, 1860.
" Here comes another letter, and not the budget I promised. The fact is, I have lost a great portion of the
verses I was to have sent you, and so shall need time and
solitude to rewrite them ; solitude being a difficult thing
to obtain amongst a party like ours, except on a fine
Sunday—a blessing we have not had for some time. I
am thinking of writing a sort of companion to the
' Summer Winds' you seem to like—I mean the exact
converse of the thoughts and character there expressed,
or meant to be. You still cling to the idea of my
thoughts, I see. I don't deny their being mine in a
certain sense, and to a certain extent ; but not necessarily. I should be very sorry to have to stand by all
the opinions I express, or rather make my imaginary
characters express, as I often speak in those poems the
thoughts of fools and rogues and madmen. I have no

character or thought of my own, in a dramatic sense. I am for the time being anybody but myself. I told you that we had found a good 'prospect' of gold ; well, we got better prospects still, and I picked a small nugget out of a drive, and we thought we had fallen on a payable patch.

We think otherwise now, but expect to strike a payable lead on a hill near. We shall know in a few days, as a shaft is bottomed there, and driving is commenced to find the bottom of the dip, where, if anywhere, the bulk of the gold will probably be. One or two of our party have lost heart and left us.

" I cannot tell you with what pleasure I look forward to the prospect of being home again. Sometimes I am kept awake half the night dreaming about it, and am obliged to begin counting a thousand to put myself asleep."

At the end of the expedition, Rowland returned home for a few months, when, led by the old spirit of adventure, he was induced to join a party which was about to proceed to the islands in the Bass Straits, for the purpose of collecting guano, which was already in great demand on the part of the farmers. So unworldly a man as Rowland was not likely to succeed in mercantile undertakings, and this one failed for various reasons, but chiefly because, when it appeared to be most promising, the Government imposed a heavy tax on guano.

The picturesque ' Log of the Sea Gull,' which will be found in the Appendix, was written at Chappell Island, where Rowland had pitched his tent.

The following extracts are from letters written at this time :

" Nothing could be more unadventurous than our life at this time ; one day was so very like another, that a record was impossible.

" When the days were warm we used occasionally to disport ourselves in the water. The natives are splendid swimmers. I have seen ' Phil Thomas,' one of the most daring boatmen in the Straits, turn a boat over and over in the water and let it fill, and then empty and right her with surprising quickness and dexterity. He had saved a good many lives, and saved, I believe, a good deal of property.

" The half-castes are, take them altogether, a fine race of people, daring and powerful, but usually indolent, as is the case with most of such tribes. Some of the women are pretty, but the hair is rather frizzly, owing to the woolly hair of the Tasmanian blacks. Those of Victoria have long straight hair. The original occupation of these islanders was sealing, but there is very little done in that business now, although there is a capital ground about forty miles from here. They live now chiefly by hunting, by the produce of sheep, and by the ' Mutton bird ' harvest.

" Animal life is very abundant in these islands, but especially bird life and reptile life. Snakes are very large and very numerous. Captain Swan told me that he and his men killed twenty-six in a two hours' walk one day. Lizards bask on the rocks in incredible numbers, to those who have not seen them—swarm indeed ; and I have several times seen scorpions in my bed, so that I used never to turn in without a strict search after these *too* friendly visitors. There is a great variety of edible birds : geese, swans, redbills, ducks, quail, &c., abound. We had a poultry yard, from which we could at any time take two or three hundred eggs. This poultry yard was a reef or island, inhabited by 'shags.' We used to go there on calm days, and the dirty, dusky-looking shags would swarm up in clouds, screaming and flapping their wings in a half-ludicrous, half-terrible fashion. I say half-terrible, because sometimes it seemed as if they would come down upon you, holus bolus, with all their filth and clamour, and drive you into the sea—fancy a death of that sort, being smothered by shags! However, the eggs are very good, rather smaller than hens' eggs, with a perfectly transparent white."

On his return home, Rowland endeavoured to construct a machine for disintegrating fibre from the wood of the gum-tree, eucalyptus, &c., so as to produce a substance resembling tow. At length he got tired of this work, and, longing for settled employment, took advantage of an interest his family had in a station in New Zealand, and having obtained influential letters of introduction, he proceeded to that colony, and obtained the appointment of town surveyor at Christchurch. It proved to be an arduous one, on account of the various conflicting opinions as to the laying out of the streets, &c. He became so much worried in his post, that he sent in his resignation, being probably the more led to do so by having fallen in with a genial companion, Mr. C. L. Money, who was exploring in search of the much coveted gold quartz. The kind of life led by them has been vividly and picturesquely described, although in simple and graphic language, in a work by Mr. Money, entitled ' Knocking about in

New Zealand.' He frequently bears testimony to the high qualities of his companion. On one occasion, when Rowley had gone away in search of provisions, he says, " My thoughts were pretty gloomy occasionally, and I pictured to myself my mate, for whom I had latterly felt a greater regard then ever, as I learnt to know and appreciate his unselfish and generous character, as having met with some accident," &c. And further on he says:—" Rowley had seen far more of life than myself, and knew its stern realities; the world no longer appeared to him as it had hitherto done to me, a pleasant place made for purposes of enjoyment only; and the experience thus gained had strengthened a naturally imaginative and poetical mind by grafting on it a definite appreciation of the real, without in the slightest degree lessening his full conception of the ideal. A more valuable companion I could not well have found ; and as you could scarcely mention the name of a work, from Boccaccio or Froissart's Chronicles to ' Verdant Green,' that he was not acquainted with, we were seldom at a loss for agreeable conversations or discussions. Doubly in his society did I enjoy scenes like that I have just described."

We shall get some glimpses of Rowland's camp life in a narrative inserted at the end of this volume, together with the following extracts, the first of which is from a letter to Mrs. Tomlinson :

" You seem surprised at the idea of my having been so long without seeing the sun ; it was not that I was at the bottom of a mine, but simply that I was living in a gorge so deep, that in the dead winter time the sun never reached its depths. I could see the golden light on the hill tops, and towards the end of our term of darkness, I could have pushed a long stick into the glory that shimmered through the birch leaves, and glowed on the ferns that draped our golden rocks. Still I was gold-digging, or rather gold-washing, up to my waist in water, with the icicles hanging from every rocky ledge, five and six feet long, clear and bright, and cold and pure, but remarkably uncomfortable.

" Now why did I lead this sort of life ? I can scarcely tell. I went out with the hope of making others' fortunes and my own. A Government party went out before us with all the appliances supposed to be necessary for an exploring party. I always kept ahead of them ; everyone of them I believe is dead, while I, thank heaven, am alive, and though old and shaky, would not shirk another expedition of a similar nature.

" You can't imagine me without books ! I think there are periods in one's life, when books seem stale, flat, and unprofitable ; one's nature seems to need action, physical action, and that only. It is astonishing how hard work, the absolute necessity of taking care of oneself, stimulates thought ; life becomes too real for books, when it takes all your skill and ingenuity, besides downright labour, to obtain something to eat. Books seem very tame, except it be everlasting books like the New Testament, ' Don Quixote,' and a few others.

" I must bring my letter to an abrupt conclusion. I can't imagine any change in you or Mr. Tomlinson. I can fancy his hair quite white, but still no change in the kind, thoughtful face ; there was something in spite of, or perhaps because of, his wisdom, almost boyish

about him ; and I hope—indeed, I am sure—there is
still.

Fragment from a New Zealand letter :

"We were encamped on a deep bank of gravel beside
the river Matakilaki ; the gravel was overgrown with a
close crisp moss, and shaded by Manuca trees, with their
stiff yet feathery foliage, white blossoms and rolls of bark
soft and brown, like a grocer's wrapping paper. The
scene was beautiful enough : mountains and wooded hills,
greenery in endless variety, and a beautiful rushing river,
swollen somewhat by rains and melted snow, for whose
subsidence we were wearily waiting. We were four
diggers out of a claim, and only waiting for the river to be
crossable to go in search of ore, or 'prospecting,' as it is
called. Our party consisted of three besides myself—one a
Welshman, an old salt and great grumbler, and inordi-
nately vain, who served not only as our private butt, but
acted in that capacity in our visits to the stores of the
digging public of our neighbourhood. I may as well call
him Jenkins. Stephen was a good-humoured cockney, a
well-educated man, and a good workman when he was at
work ; but as long as he had a shilling in his pocket, or
there was a glass of grog to be had, he would idle about
the stores. Roberts was a tall man of Kent, who had
held a commission in a fast regiment, but was now,
and had been for years, a hard working and speculating
digger. I had myself only recently joined the party,
though Roberts and I had been friends for some time.
Several times we had attempted the river without success,
finding the water too strong ; however, at last, one fine
Monday morning we took down our tent, and 'swagged
up,' determined to cross at all hazards. Stephen having a
lame leg, we despatched him to the stores, which, miserable 'shanties' though they were, served for hospital,
hotel, library, and all sorts of purposes. We crossed the

river on two streams: the first was deep and rough, but we had all clung on to a stick, so that in the event of one being taken off his legs, the other two would probably be able to keep him up. This is the Maori method of wading rivers ; the first man breaks the rush of water, and the other keeps him up. It is astonishing the force of water that three or four men can withstand in this way. The second stream we waded separately, and all arrived on the south bank of the Matakilaki with our luggage, about 70 or 80 lbs. per man, without accident. Penetrating a narrow belt of bush, we began to cross a plain covered with thistles and fern, and fringed with a great pine forest, the open dotted with little islands of shrubs, and crossed with winding belts of scrub. Crossing the open we managed to strike a digger's path leading through the pine forest, the shade of which was very grateful, as the day was very hot and our swags abominably heavy."

After separating from Mr. Money, Rowland became engineer to a gold-digging party on Lyell's Creek, Buller River, from the mouth of which they had to draw their supplies. Rowland was a good oarsman, and generally accompanied the supply party, and on one occasion during the return passage, no sooner had they reached the mouth of the creek when they found it swollen by heavy rains, so that the water was rushing down like a boiling torrent. The steersman called out " Pull ! pull ! " when, as Rowland says,' " we did pull for our lives, and by God's help we saved them ; for we had just got through the rapid, when the canoe was upset. I had caught hold of it, and feared I was alone, but presently all my companions were seen clinging to the frail bark, when to our dismay an eddy was seen approaching us ; but happily, help came from the shore, on which we were soon safely landed, minus everything but the clothes we had on. I had some sketches and verses for you, also notes of travel, but they are all gone, as well as our stores. This is Christmas, my unlucky time, and yet how happy in being saved ! "

Shortly after this accident, he again returned home, and early in 1866 obtained employment under Government in the public works, which he held for fifteen months, at the end of which time the staff of officers in this department was reduced, and Rowland, being the last to join, was the first to be dismissed. The head of the department wrote a warm testimonial in his favour. His duties while in this employment exposed him very much to the weather in an open boat, the effect of which was to produce a painful affection of the eyes, which nearly deprived him of sight. Rest, change of air, and medicine failed to relieve him, so that he determined to proceed to Sydney to visit his old friend and fellow-student, Dr. Fortescue. He was received by him with brotherly affection, lodged in his own house, and treated so skilfully, that his sight was soon restored.

On his return to Tasmania, he hoped for occupation on the proposed main line railway. In the meantime he took an office in Hobart, and succeeded in obtaining some employment, but, as far as the railway was concerned, he was engaged in nothing further than a preliminary survey. The work of his office not being sufficient to maintain him, he set out on an expedition in search of gold, to Fingal, near Ben Lomond, but he found that nothing could be done without powerful and costly machinery.

The following letter was written from Hobart about this time :

"DEAR MRS. TOMLINSON,

"You must forgive my long silence—the more that the loss has been mine—but indeed I have written to no one but my mother for the last three or four years, and to her but seldom ; indeed, my way of life made it impossible for me to keep up any correspondence. On my return home, I found photographs of yourself and Mr. Tomlinson, which would have recalled you perfectly to me, had I needed any such aids to memory ; time seems to have made no change in you. I used to hear of you often from my mother—of your good works, your noble life, and your kind thoughts of me. I have had the pleasure of reading your last letter, giving, amongst other things, an account of some pictures in the Royal Academy. I envy nothing in your English life, more than your access to those great treasures of art, which yearly adorn your many galleries. I generally read the criticisms in your newspapers, but they are for the most part written more for people who see them, than for us who do not see the pictures they describe. Your descriptions, on the other hand, enable me to realise the pictures as well, I think even better in some respects, than a photograph or engraving. Mr. Tomlinson's dictum, that one cannot paint a metaphor, has struck me much. I am not sure that I agree with him, but I will think it out. Of late years I have been wholly cut off from art. I have had great opportunities of studying nature, and have often tried to beguile loneliness and to heighten my interest in the scenery around me, by trying to systematise the forms of the chief objects in nature, and to determine what constitutes beauty in inanimate nature, and the relation of that beauty to art and to ourselves.

" It must be very pleasant to be an artist—to have work at once a work, a worship, and a love. With most of us our work is an obligation, not a joy ; though any sort of work is better than none, and I suppose none are so miserable as those who do nothing, and know it.

" I hear that Mr. Tomlinson has been working harder than ever in fresh fields of science, and gaining fresh laurels as a discoverer of new and strange facts ; however, I have been as much out of the way of science as of art, so only know these things by hearsay."

As a mark of the respect in which Rowland was held by all who knew him, he was invited by the residents of the Channel and Huon to become a candidate for their vacant seat in Parliament. He went among them and took some steps in that direction, but eventually retired in favour of an older and more influential man.

In 1872 Rowland revisited Victoria, shortly after which his father, who had gone to New Zealand on business, asked him to join him there, which he did, and through the interest of influential friends again succeeded in obtaining employment, which occupied him for about a year, when he was again overtaken by what he called his usual ill-luck. In a letter to

his mother, dated Wellington, September 1873, he
says :

" I went out one fine morning with only a linen shirt,
instead of the usual Crimean. As it happened, it came on
a bitter south-easter with sleety showers. I suppose I
got a chill, for when I came home I had no appetite,
though I had neither ' bite nor sup ' all day from breakfast till the first public in Wellington, when my man and
I had a glass of beer. Well, I went to bed about eight
o'clock to pass a day or two of ague. After that I awoke in
the night with a sensation of choking, and found my mouth
full of blood, which kept flowing without intermission for
twenty-four hours or more : then I kept swallowing the
blood and went off in a sort of faint ; in fact, I thought I
was dying. However, I got about next day, but in the
evening off I went again in a sort of faint or fit ; anyway, I
was insensible for some time. The people were alarmed,
and went for the doctor. Well, after a little I became con-
valescent, but then on came acute pains in my head, all
my teeth got sore, so that I could eat nothing solid, and
could speak only with great difficulty. Well, this went
away, my face swelling, of course ; then I thought I was
rid of it, when on it came as it used to in England, right
across my eyes, and kept on a long time. Had it lasted
much longer, I must have lost my senses. As it was, I
almost seemed unable to think, and it was quite impossible to enter into the calculations necessary to render
the portion of my work completed, of use to my employers. Meanwhile, I regained my appetite and fat, so
looked well enough, except for my eyes. As I said before,
people never believe a fat florid fellow can be ill."

" That illness of mine has done me a great deal of harm,
I have lost my work thereby—work which would have
led to more, had I been able to complete it. The worst
of it is, employers lose confidence in one."

We need not be surprised that on the receipt of such news, Rowland's parents ordered him home, not only on account of his health, but that of the death of a married sister and the engagement of his second sister, which made the presence of their only son still more necessary to them. He had so far recovered his health as to be on the point of accepting a lucrative post in New Zealand, but he obeyed his parents' wish, and they were glad to see him again, looking bright and happy. He had long been attached to a lady who knew how to appreciate him, and in January 1875, they were married by his father. They took possession of a little cottage belonging to his parents, and close to their home. It was in a retired spot, commanding a pleasant view, with a glimpse of the river Derwent. while Rowland's dear old mountain was to be seen from one end of the house. The cottage was surrounded by flower-beds, which the young wife loved to cultivate ; and as the position was many feet above Ferndene, these flower-beds presented a blaze of colour in approaching the house. The one sitting-room, adorned with pictures and flowers, arranged in exquisite taste, and the nameless grace which pervades a room where a lady presides, contributed to soothe and charm Rowland's artistic taste.

The following notes by Mrs. Rowland Davies will give some idea of their too few years of married life :

E

Of their married life his wife says :—" There is so little to tell ; we were so evenly and quietly happy, ever preferring the pleasures of our dear small home, our books, readings of Browning, Wordsworth, &c., and our long rambles and explorations, to that of society, the enjoyments of which must soon have been foregone, as his health began to decline more and more each year. We sought in change its restoration, and in a certain measure for some time with good result, but disease was too surely there. He used to say, if he could only go on one of his long bush expeditions, he would be sure to get well again. I can look back to my first experience of 'roughing it ' when I used to accompany him, for the benefit of sea air, to many of the small 'settlements ' down the channel ; his enjoyment while there was so thorough, he was for ever exploring, taking the whole day to wander off far away in the wilds. He was so happy and in such buoyant spirits on these trips to the sea-side, to which, but for his society I had the strongest objection. The small passage boats, the only way really of reaching these remote spots (except that of going overland, over horrible bush roads), were to me very unpleasant ; they are used, I believe, only for bringing timber and produce up to Hobart, and taking down provisions ; passengers are taken too. I remember upon one occasion the boat seemed to me to ride upon her side, while the waves dashed over us. Our lodgings in any of the places we visited were always clean, and I think, when I have said that, I can add nothing more to recommend them, except the great grand fires we used to have. To Rowley, however, everything was enjoyable, and his great sense of the ridiculous made things endurable to him which to me were very trying. Of a little room we occupied, hung round with coarse framed prints, he speaks, writing to his mother: ' We have a very nice little room, good fires, two or three shepherdesses, the " Oxford and Cambridge boat-races "

St. Peter with a very white beard making an exhibition of
himself in the water, and several other prints of the
Roman persuasion.'

" It was in 1877 that we used to seek in Tasmania the
change so necessary for my husband ; but in 1878 it was
thought that a trip to Victoria would be more beneficial.
He was suffering from great debility and an affection of
the brain, the result of sunstroke. There in the great
bright city we passed a large portion of the winter, and
with renewed health he was able to enjoy all there was to
be seen ; the galleries of art and the theatres were his
special pleasures, his knowledge of art enabling me the
more to appreciate all I saw. He had such a wonderful
way of imparting his great stores of knowledge ; so much
enthusiasm and animation, and flow of language. I
remember so well his special gift of '*Speechifying*'
which he loved to ' air' on all our family grand occasions—on his father's or mother's birth or wedding days.
The easy grace of his manner, the tenderness which at one
moment caused our eyes to suffuse with tears, and the
charming pleasantry which at another would excite our
laughter just like an April day, ' all smiles and tears.' "

About 1880 Rowland's health gradually grew worse,
and the fainting fits which followed the breaking of a
blood-vessel in New Zealand were accompanied by
slight epileptic attacks, which became rather frequent,
but yielded to treatment. He went to Melbourne for
change of air, and soon rallied sufficiently to enjoy
that city and Clunes. After six weeks' absence, he
returned home, better in health, but the disease was
only checked for a time, and he often suffered greatly.
Giddiness came on at times, so that he was obliged to

ride home, being, as he said, ashamed to be seen in
the streets, lest the cause of his unsteady walk should
be mistaken. In the beginning of 1880, his father
became a confirmed invalid, and Rowland and his
wife frequently visited him for the purpose of cheering
and amusing him. As he became worse they took up
their abode in the house, which was a great comfort
to both parents. On the death of the Archdeacon
other relations arrived, and Rowland and his wife
returned to their cottage. Rowland continued to get
worse, but his tender regard for his mother was such
that after passing a night of suffering, as was too often
the case, he would say to his wife, " Don't tell my
mother." He had often remarked years before, ere
his health had begun to wane, that he should not live
long after forty ; but after recovering from his illnesses,
he said he believed he had taken a new lease of life
and should live yet some years ; that he would go to
Launceston, where, being nearer to the mining districts,
he would find plenty of employment, and obtain more
information for a ' Mining Journal' that he had
projected. " We will get a cottage ready," he said,
" and you must come, mother dear, and live in my
home, and we shall be so happy." He went to
Launceston, and obtained the additional information
that he required, and on his return, on the 6th of July,
he was much occupied in getting through the press
the first number of his journal, combating the many

unexpected hindrances that arose. The keen interest
he felt in this work caused him to neglect the symptoms
which appeared on two successive days, and on his
return home on the evening of Saturday, the 9th, his
exertions made him feel languid and unwell. On
Sunday morning he was much worse, though his
medical attendant did not think his case very serious.
In the evening the internal hæmorrhage, which had
been checked during the morning hours, again broke
out, and he suffered much from exhaustion. He
often talked of death, and some days before it came to
him, he remarked cheerfully that death was only the
beginning of another and a better life, though he did
not know what kind of a life it would be. Only three
evenings before he passed away, he seemed so weary
that his mother and wife wished him to go to bed
early, but he said, "I will stay up to read prayers for
my mother; I should like to do so before I go." He
passed quietly away to a higher life on Monday, the
11th, eight months after the death of his father, by
whose side his remains rest in St. John's Cemetery,
New Town.

We cannot do better than close this notice with the
following extract from a paper written for the purpose
of this memoir, and entitled 'A Day with Rowland
Davies,' by his friend and companion, the Rev. H. D.
Atkinson.

The two had been camping out in the Bush in

the autumn of 1870, in the most beautiful part of Tasmania, D'Entrecasteaux Channel :

" Mountains wooded to the summit appear on every side, some snow-clad for more than half the year ; numerous islands dot the surface of the water ; and the changing panorama, as you round a fresh point in your boat, and look up and down the fiord-like bays, has to be seen once, never to be forgotten.

" Rowland arrived one evening in a barge, and at once made himself at home in the bush ; in fact, being a man of versatile temperament, he quickly made himself at home anywhere, and I never saw him in the society to which he could not adapt himself. But although a man well fitted to adorn the more refined social gatherings of either sex, to me he always seemed the best, because the happiest, in 'the bush.' I think of him sitting in the opening in our little tent, on a bunch of withered fern, his face bronzed with the sun, and radiant with good humour. He had a pleasant laugh and a ready joke at all times, and would occasionally pour out his astonishing fund of literary knowledge, with a happy freedom that seemed wanting on more sedate occasions.

" The morning after Rowland's arrival I missed him, and as he did not respond to the usual cooey, I went in search of him. He had wandered along the pebbly beach of Hearne Bay, and was found standing close to the edge of the water, watching the gulls and tern as they floated motionless inshore, and further away the voracious gannets, as they dived for their early breakfast. He was slowly repeating aloud those sad but beautiful ' Lines ' of Shelley's, ' written in dejection near Naples.' Perhaps he found something congenial in the prospect ; perhaps the association of feeling came from within. To me the scene was one of unmixed beauty. The main direction of the channel was here hidden, and the part seen looked

like a vast lake, calm and peaceful. There was no cloud
in the sky, and a gentle breeze off-shore just rippled the
water into little dancing wavelets. All over the Bruné
Hills every object was marvellously distinct, and a
general air of repose pervaded the scene. Even the
birds seemed at rest—all except the swift gannets flashing about in every attitude of motion, now rising and
again falling with a plunge after their finny prey. But
they were far out, and rather added to the beauty of the
view. All was peaceful and still where we were, under
the overhanging trees ; behind, a magnificent forest
spread upwards to the summit of Mount Royal, and the
sun just peeping over the Bruné Hills began to warm the
cool autumn air. But I could only sympathise with poor
Rowland's despondency, for he had been ill and debarred
from any kind of active work. So, while walking back
together, I thought of a little plan of amusement for him,
and during breakfast proposed that we should have a
ramble on Bruné and a night's 'camping out.' Rowland
seemed pleased with the idea ; so we at once hastened to
make our preparations. A fine whale-boat I had was
got ready ; tent, blankets, and provisions were stowed
away ; also a net and cooking utensils ; and a third man,
in case of bad weather, was easily persuaded to make one
of the party. The day was still young when we found
ourselves standing away from the little settlement, with
all our canvas set to the freshening breeze. The western
shore gradually receded, and the lake-like appearance of
the channel quickly changed ; we could see southward
full twenty miles, and much further off *La Pérouse*, with
his serried crags all hidden in snow.

"We had a beautiful sail. Rounding 'Simpson's Point'
we came in full view of the 'neck,' a long ridge of sand,
which unites the two Brunés, widening out to meet the
islands at either end, and tapering off in the middle to
some hundred yards' width, where the prevailing winds,

in past ages, have raised three enormous hummocks, the largest in the centre, now all covered with 'epacris' and stunted 'banksias.' We made for the lower end of the 'neck,' hoping to find deeper water, but it shoaled at a good distance away ; so we were compelled to anchor our boat, and wade to shore, carrying our impedimenta. Rowland's spirits rose rapidly with the excitement, and we had many a hearty laugh as we plodded knee-deep in the water. Huge stinging rays darted away from our feet. A few stray oysters could be seen here and there, and thousands of sea-birds wheeled and screamed overhead. We at length reached the low bushes that overhang the beach, and soon found a beautiful place to camp under the gum trees, about the middle of the 'neck.' Firewood lay all around, and a spring of fresh water was close at hand. And now all was bustle. To one was assigned the work of cutting poles and setting up the tent, another got armfuls of withered grass for the bed, and a third prepared for the important work of slinging the 'billy.' We soon did justice to a second breakfast, and then the question arose, How were we to spend the day ? Rowland declared himself equal to any exertion ; so we strolled through the low trees across the neck and came on the beach of Adventure Bay, in the corner of which Cook careened his ship the *Adventure*—hence the name. Here were no sheltering islands, the wide Pacific rolled in from the south-east with a sullen roar. Yet the view was grand. Away to the north stood the huge masses of stratified rock that guard the entrance of the bay, while beyond them rose the precipitous walls of 'Cape Raoul,' or 'Tasman's Peninsula.' At the other extremity of the bay, 'Fluted Cape' reared its gigantic head 900 feet above the sea level. To right and left stretched the firm beach in a wide sweep of many miles. Rowland was greatly interested with Fluted Cape, and declared that we ought to go to the very top of it—it looked so majestic, and above all, so near. But I was doubtful about his ability to stand the fatigue, for the distance was really much greater than he supposed. We were looking at it across the corner of the bay—along what geometers would call the chord of the arc ; the *length* of the arc, which we should be compelled to traverse, with its frequent gullies and unknown track, was a different matter. But the prospect of getting where, with all my wanderings, I had never ventured, was too great to be resisted. Anyway, we could stop and come back if we got tired. So after securing something by way of lunch to eat, if we succeeded in reaching the summit, we started off with the exuberant spirits of schoolboys out for a holiday.

" It is needless to describe the particulars of the journey. It was up hill and down, through blind creeks and tangled scrub, and everywhere rough laborious walking. However, after some three hours of continuous exertion, we came out of the timbered country on to the little beach which lies near the foot of the Cape. We quickly traversed this, wading through the creek that passes over it, and after resting awhile at the foot of the slope, we began the ascent by the easiest grade we could find. Fortune seemed to favour us, for after half-an-hour's pretty stiff climbing, we found ourselves at the goal of our journey, and at once threw ourselves down on the short grass, very proud of our victory, but with little breath to proclaim it aloud. Low ' she-oak ' and ' cherry ' trees occur all over the Cape, and project over its precipitous edge. Hanging on to these, and sometimes crawling quite flat, we peeped over the beetling cliff, down its vast height, upon the boulders at the base where the mighty waves churned themselves into foam ; but no faintest sound of the tumult reached our ears. It was a grand but fearful sight, and one seldom seen, for the country is all uninhabited. Looking down, we could trace the huge columns of prismatic greenstone, that rose hundreds of feet along the face of the cliff like vast chimneys, on which, at varying heights, perched innumerable cormorants. I began to think of the lines in 'King Lear,' and of the "choughs and crows that winged the midway air,' and I asked Rowland if it reminded him of 'Shakspere's Cliff'; but he gazed downwards and said nothing. After a moment I found he had crawled carefully backward, as if overcome by the dizzy view, and on my regaining his place of safety, he said, 'I heard you quite well, but I could not speak; "Shakspere's Cliff" is nothing to that. What an awful sight! I never imagined anything like it.'

"We stayed but a short time, eating our lunch rapidly, enjoying the while the glorious view, and then we began the descent, which was easy enough, and prepared for the toilsome tramp back to camp. I led the way homewards, feeling that we had not a moment to lose, as it would be a joke, neither contemplated nor likely to be enjoyed, to be benighted in the bush, away from tent and provisions. But by dint of hard steady walking, we reached our camp safely just as the sun was setting. I was afraid the rough walk of over twenty miles would not prove very good medicine for my sick friend, especially as I had been compelled to force the pace towards the finish of our journey; but I was mistaken. He was in the best of spirits; I could hardly believe him to be the same man: for no trace of his morning's despondency remained; the transformation effected by the pure air, exertion, and fresh scenery, was complete. Tired as he must have been, he set to work building up the fire, whereat we toasted unnumbered slices of bacon, and drank large pannikins of tea, which Rowland declared was the most delicious beverage he had ever tasted. 'It was nectar fit for the gods,' he said. I never knew him so happy, never so vivacious, sparkling, and amiable. He was full of anecdote and conversation, and we laughed long and loudly.

"Oh, what a happy rest! we sat on our blankets with our feet to the fire till far into the night: till every star in the Southern host had looked down upon us ; until the last frog croaked in the marshy ground. The ring-tailed oppossums ran up and down the smooth boles of the peppermint trees, the wild ducks all came back to the lagoon from their last forage along the shore ; the bats made their final inaudible gyrations, before we turned into the tent. And a tent was barely needed ; for, surrounded on all sides by the sea, the air was never cold, but we slept on, regardless of temperature, until the sun was high amongst the tree tops. Then more bacon, tea. and laughter. But why should I continue? Let it suffice to say. I never enjoyed a night in the bush more, although many pleasant 'campings out' have been celebrated in other parts of the colony.

"It was a pleasure to be with Rowland Davies, away from the haunts of men. Every voice of nature spoke to him, and he never failed to interpret any of her utterances. The journey home again need not be described, for I only began to speak of 'a day with Rowland Davies,'—a rash promise in itself, for the attempt to reproduce the effects of beautiful scenery such as we had is generally a failure ; and I am sure no words could faithfully give an impression of our conversation. Rowland's ideas always seemed novel and unexpected, yet, after reflection, they were found just, and most happily expressed. His fluency was unsurpassed. When excited, his words flowed in a perfect torrent of utterance : they were so rapid and incisive, that it was impossible to apprehend them in the time given for conversation. Yet, with all his sharp and bright sayings, I never knew him to use an expression that could have jarred on the most sensitive ear ; and although he had plenty of humour, he had little or no sarcasm. He was essentially an amiable man, and usually took the kindest view that was possible of men and things.

"There can be little doubt that Rowland mistook his profession : civil engineering, however attractive, from a scientific or industrial standpoint, was too dull and mechanical for a mind like his. He was essentially a man of letters ; and literature, in some form, should have been the work of his life. I have seen him throw off a copy of verses without any apparent effort. He wrote rapidly, as he spoke, and it was seldom needful to alter a word. He was familiar with every English author of note, and although I thought I knew Shakspere pretty well, a conversation with my friend showed me that my acquaintance with the great dramatist was mostly verbal and literary. I remember his psychological criticism of Hamlet, and how he could appreciate the beauties and even the defects of that masterpiece. He also knew the entire English drama equally well. Amongst the moderns, perhaps his favourite authors were Wordsworth and Browning ; his liking for the former being, no doubt, prompted by his love of nature. In disposition, Rowland Davies was a shy man, and not prone to be communicative with strangers. He required to be known, and, probably for this reason, was sometimes misunderstood. He evidently liked my society, and I should have been dull indeed not to have valued his ; for it was a treat to hear him speak in his best moods, though he was always amiable and gentlemanly in manner.

"Not very long after our excursion to the ' Neck,' and ' Fluted Cape,' I left that part of Tasmania, and lost sight of my friend and the romantic scenery of the island at the same time, and then I heard of his continual illness, and shortly the news came of his death. I felt greatly moved by this, partly because he had always been my friend, and more because I felt that the future I had always expected him to achieve for himself would now never become a reality. I look upon him as the most original thinker I have ever known in Tasmania."

POEMS.

POEMS.

A DIRGE.

(Written at the age of sixteen.)

BRING me a shroud
    White as a cloud,
That silvers the azure sky ;
    For oh ! she is dead,
    In her lonely bed,
Where she for ever must lie.

    By sorrow shaded,
    Her loveliness faded,
As fadeth a thirsting flower,
    Which droops away
    On a summer day,
For the love of a dewy shower.

    Then bring her a shroud,
    White as the cloud

That silvers yon azure sky;
 For alas ! she is dead,
 In her lonely bed,
Where she for ever must lie.

 Let music be played
 O'er the grave where she's laid,
Which as lightly may fall on the ear,
 As falls, at the blight
 Of her dreams of delight,
A maiden's pearly tear.

 No emblem of gloom
 Should o'ershadow the tomb
Where so lovely a maiden is sleeping ;
 But flowerets fair
 Should be planted there,
Like angels their vigils keeping.

 Then bring her a shroud
 White as the cloud,
Which silvers yon azure sky ;
 For alas ! she is dead,
 In her lonely bed,
Where she for ever must lie.

FOREST RAMBLES.

I.

WHEN spring seemed to rest in the arms of the
summer,
As loth to part from the bright new comer,
I strolled along through the forest aisles,
Wandering on for miles and miles :
I went through many a dim arcade,
Which covered the path with its dark green shade,
Save here and there, where the sun peered through.
And gave me a glimpse of the heaven's blue.
The foliage had every tint of green
That the eye so loves in a forest scene ;
And the leaves, when pluck'd and press'd to the palm,
Emitted an odour of myrrh and balm.
On every side there were beautiful bowers
Where one might lie on a mat of flowers,
And dream away all the noontide hours ;
There were endless mazes that twisted about,
With a thousand turnings in and out,
And the boughs above all intertwining,
Made twilight there while the sun was shining ;

F

And flowers grew there so very fair,
That they seemed almost to be born of air ;
And pendulous berries of white and red
Hung from the branches overhead.

I found my way into dark recesses,
Where parasites hung like dishevelled tresses,
That fall like a veil o'er a lady's face,
Hiding a beauty, but adding a grace ;
And these recesses, thus veiled from sight,
Admitting only a solemn light,
Seemed a shrine that was set apart
For man to worship his God in heart ;
Shrines in a temple of glorious size,
Whose floor is the earth, and whose dome the skies.

I turned aside into rocky dells,
All indented with mossy cells,
Beautiful elfin palaces,
Where sprites and fairies may take their ease.
Lichens hung down from each vaulted roof—
Tapestries woven in nature's woof,
And the flowers had carpets of softest mosses,
Bestrewn with cushions and velvet bosses.
Sometimes a stream would dash down the dell,
And wherever its glistening waters fell,
And scooped in the rock a bubbling well,
There clouds of insects of every hue—
Red and golden, and purple and blue—

Were coming and going and coming again,
Like wingèd thoughts through a dreamer's brain.

I went far down into caverns dim,
Where the water was singing its passionless hymn,
Gushing on with a crisp, clear sound
Which awakened the echoes that dwelt underground ;
And beautiful pendulous stalactites fell
From a roof that was dark and invisible ;
Some were so airy, so thin and slight,
As to seem like frozen beams of light ;
And some had the forms of stranger things
Than ever my wild imaginings
Had pictured to me in my noonday dreams ;
And others there were bestarred with the gleams
Of countless glow-worms, whose gem-like light
Made them faintly and softly bright,
Yet indistinct as a morning mist,
That is hued with the sapphire and amethyst.
The floor beneath seemed paved with snow,
Petrified long ages ago,
But still retaining the roseate tint
And the golden hue that marked the print
Of the passionate kiss of the burning sun
Ere he sank to rest when the day was done.

And so through the cavern I onward went,
My senses dazzled with wonderment,

Till at last I came by another way,
Once more to the breezy light of day.
I found myself in an open glade,
Where noble trees threw a partial shade,
While the sun streamed down in golden patches,
Like melody heard by fits and snatches ;
And about and around these trees there grew
Delicate flowers of every hue,
Bright and clear on the dusky ground,
Like voices we love on an ocean of sound ;
And though the trees were so grand and tall,
I loved the flowers better than all.
I often stopped as I strolled along,
To listen awhile to the wild birds' song ;
For dear to me is the singing of birds,
It speaks to my heart like burning words,
Till my brain is fraught with all kinds of fancies,
Bright and swift as a maiden's glances.
I often sat in sequestered nooks,
That were filled with the sound of gushing brooks
Now loud as a wind 'mid echoing trees,
Now dying away into cadences ;
While the scent of the plants that grew around
Came wafted along on the waves of sound,
Till a slumb'rous pleasure the most intense
Brought every feeling and every sense
To bow to its magic influence,
And Sleep threw a veil athwart my eyes,

Till I saw no earth, till I saw no skies :
And he gave me to drink of a magic bowl
Which brought sweet visions to gladden my soul.
How long I slept I do not know,
But when I awoke the sun was low,
And wrote on the scroll that the clouds unrolled,
In letters of crimson, in letters of gold,
Wrote with a swift unerring finger,
The doom of the day that fain would linger,
If only to see the sable Night
Come sweeping on in her gentle might.

II.

WHEN the summer was dead, one sultry day,
To the self-same forest I went my way ;
But summer had kindled a raging fire,
And the forest had made her funeral pyre.
So all was burnt, and every breath
Of air was rank with the smell of death :
Though some of the trees were standing still,
Which the fire might injure but could not kill,
And blackened and burnt they rose to the sky,
As seeking vengeance from One on high.
But all beneath was black and bare,
All burnt and charred that was once so fair ;
And nothing but ashes could now be seen,
Where beautiful woods had lately been,

Delighting my soul with their emerald sheen.
And the forest children, the pearl-eyed flowers,
That were nursed and reared in jewelled bowers,
And the velvet moss, and the delicate grass,
Lay burnt and dead in one desolate mass.

I sought for the caves ; but their entrances
Were covered up by the fallen trees,
And the stream within, if it ran at all,
Must have gushed along with a sorrowful fall,
Not loud as a singing, but rather a sighing,
A muttered dirge for the dead and dying.

I turned aside into rocky dells,
And looked again at the rock-built cells ;
The beautiful, fairy-like, elfin homes
That now were merely the catacombs
Of countless delicate fragile things—
Of lichens, and shells, and butterflies' wings,
Of numberless insects bright and fair,
Which had fled from the fire for safety there ;
But the treacherous smoke with her stifling breath
Had wantonly put every one to death.

I tried, but all in vain, to hear
The wild birds' songs that were wont to cheer
My soul, as they sang the trees among,
Till I thought that the very spirit of song
From the trembling trees and the panting skies

Was uttering exquisite melodies.
But now, alas! there was no such singing,
No music now in the forest ringing ;
No echoing notes of joy and gladness,
No tremulous dying wail of sadness ;
For vanished had all the sweet wild quire,
At the first low hiss of the creeping fire ;
And the nearest bird was so very far,
That it seemed in its flight like a falling star.

In vain I sought for the green recesses—
In vain for the leafy lonelinesses,
Within whose shade I was wont to lie
And gaze, with a dreamy, half-shut eye,
For hours together into the sky,
Which peeped through every cranny and chink,
Till at last I would sometimes almost think
That angels' eyes of the deepest blue
Were looking at me the green leaves through.

In vain I sought for the forest glades,
The arching valleys and dim arcades,
Wherein I did so love to stroll,
When I wanted thoughts to soothe my soul ;
For there was ever a gentle quiet,
No jarring noise, no grating riot,
No sound more loud than the rustle of boughs
That answered the breezes' whispered vows.
But all these places were swept away,

On the buried summer's funeral day,
And all around was bare and black—
Not a stone but spoke of the fire's track.
The streams that once with a rhyming sound
Had plashed like rain on the glittering ground,
Were dammed and choked by fallen logs,
A refuge for serpents, and toads, and frogs,
Which now and then the stillness broke,
With the loathsome sound of their dismal croak;
And on all these pools, from bank to bank,
A shiny covering, green and dank,
Grew over the whole till the waters stank.
There was nothing to move, nothing to stir,
In all that gloomy sepulchre;
The horrible stillness everywhere
Filled the sky and the dreary air,
And the earth seemed but one stagnant ocean,
Destitute of life and motion.

So everything that I saw was dead,
And my soul was filled with a morbid dread—
A horror of something undefined—
So that I dared not look behind,
For fear I might see some terrible thing,
Which my brain meanwhile was imagining.
I trembled with fear at the slightest sound
Of my feet as they fell on the crumbling ground:
Nay, I scarcely dared to draw my breath,

For it seemed to me as the whisper of death.
But in time this horror wore away,
Though I felt so lonely I could not stay;
And I strangely longed to hear again
The familiar speech of my fellow men;
For a voice, though of rudest and harshest tone,
Would have made me feel not all alone.

And now, as I felt the rain and the sleet,
Seeming to me like the unseen beat
And the wingèd sound of an angel's feet;
Like steps of memory touching the heart
That hath long been dead or living apart,
Rousing the soul from its dream of care,
And that desolate, deadly sleep, despair—
So my soul grew glad when I heard the rain,
For I knew that the forest would rise again.

A DAY DREAM.

———◆———

ONCE in the musing twilight
　　Of advancing summer day,
I sat at my window gazing
　　On the landscape far away ;
Thinking sadly, dreaming madly,
　　Of a bright and fair young maiden
Who should have been my bride :
　　Of a fair and beauteous maiden
Who should have been my bride,
　　With her throbbing hand in mine,
Sitting gladly at my side.

But ah ! she was too beautiful
　　For such a one as I !
The very demons loved her,
　　And the angels in the sky ;
And so at last it happened
　　That the spirit we call Death,
Came one balmy summer evening,
　　And kissed away her breath ;
O God ! that I were Death !

And thus, as I was floating
  On the ebb of memory's stream,
Never marking, never noting
  Aught else beside my dream,
Suddenly I heard a ringing
  Of a strange aerial singing,
Of a wild unearthly singing,
  Throughout my chamber ringing,
With its ghostly melody.

Half startled from my slumbers
By these wild extatic numbers,
  I turned me round to see
Whose voice it was thus singing
The strains that were so ringing
  With their wondrous melody.
But neither maid nor lady,
  As I thought it might have been,
Nor demon, saint, nor angel,
  Could anywhere be seen,

Though the music still continued
  Like the music heard in dreams ;
Like the midnight wail of breezes,
  And the gushing sound of streams.
And I saw that in the harpsichord
  The key notes rose and fell,
As moved by the swift fingers
  Of some form invisible.

And I gazed with strange deep longing
　　Into the empty air,
Half expecting and half fearing
　　To see an angel there ;
Till scarcely with my senses,
　　But rather with my mind,
I saw at first a brightness
　　Indistinct and undefined.
Then a shape all rainbow coloured,
　　Seemed to grow beneath my sight,
Like a first fair beam of daybreak
　　Growing out of night.

Till at last I saw a radiant soul
　　In a mist of amber light,
The glorified soul of my lost love
Whom Death had ta'en to realms above,
　　Leaving the angels to visit me,
And to soothe my heart in its misery ;
　　But the beauty and the glory,
And the radiance so intense,
　　For several moments dazzled
Every thought and every sense.

"Surely this is no more dreaming,
　　Surely, surely I have died,
And wake to live for ever
　　With thee, my radiant bride !"

So saying, I rushed forwards
  To clasp her to my breast,
But alas ! the barren empty air
  Was all my closed arms prest.
Though a passionate piercing pleasure
  Rushed through my trembling frame,
And my brain grew dim with madness
Of joy, and over gladness.
Meanwhile the ghostly singing,
With its wild and passionate ringing,
  Filled the panting air.
Till at last, like an echo sighing,
I heard it dying, dying,
  Dying gently in the air.
Though long ago I ceased to hear
That music sounding in my ear,
Yet in my heart ' tis sweet and clear.
Yes, it lingers, ever lingers,
The seraph music of those fingers,
And her angel weirdlike singing
Still is ringing, still is ringing
To my lonely spirit clinging
  Like a memory of gladness ;
And the thought of that bright maiden
Soothes my soul that's overladen,
  With its load of grief and sadness,
Filling my heart with joy and peace
That cannot lessen, never cease.

(1855.)

THE LOVER'S RIDE.

WITH unchecked bit and slackened rein,
 I madly gallop across the plain,
And the yielding turf has a springy feel,
As my horse bounds on in fiery zeal.

I scarcely mark the beauteous scene,
Though the gums are dressed in their brightest green,
And the wattle-boughs, laden with golden bloom,
Fill the air with a sweet perfume.

For I only think of the weary miles
That I must ride, ere I see the smiles
Of one beloved, who will welcome me
To our pleasant home by the sounding sea.

But alas! I feel that my jaded steed
Slackens by slow degrees his speed,
Yet, as I live, I will never stop,
Though weariness make him ready to drop.

No! by the God who rules above,
I will not stay till the one I love,
With her gentle smile, hath welcomed me
To our pleasant home by the sounding sea.

Home with the spurs still deeper in,
Till blood pours down from his wounded skin,
And the ruby stream has already dyed
The spotless white of each reeking side.

Aha ! there is life in those drops of gore !
Madly we gallop along once more :
He seems to know I have sworn a vow,
For his pace is wilder than ever now.

Hurrah ! hurrah ! we have gained the shore !
How joyous to me is the ocean's roar !
It speaks of the smiles that will welcome me
To our pleasant home by the sounding sea.

But where can she be ? Ever before
She has strolled to meet me upon the shore !
Best God ! how they wail, the wind and the sea !
I could almost fancy they spake to me.

Where art thou, Ellēna, my love, my bride ?
Is thy welcome smile to my soul denied ?
Ah ! I know what they say, the wind and the sea :
Never more, never more will she welcome thee.

I look through the window, and on the bed
I see her form, but cold and dead ;
I feel it is Death, as I sadly trace
The heavenly smile on her pallid face,

The angel smile on her angel face.
And I know what they say, the wind and the sea :
" She smiles on heaven, and not on thee."

With a snort of terror, again my steed
Bounds away at a ghostly speed,
And on, still on I am forced to ride,
Though I fain would stay by my dead young bride.

Years are passing, and changes come,
Grief to the many, and joy to some ;
But we change not, my steed and I,
And alas ! alas ! we can never die.

Still on we must ride till the last great day,
When heaven and earth shall pass away,
And my bride will come to welcome me,
Fulfilling my vow, and setting me free.

(1855.)

JOY AND SORROW.

THE sweetest things have ever been the saddest.
  Mere joy hath nothing half so exquisite.
So dying sweet, as sorrow.   It is to joy
As loveliness to beauty.   Joy is a rose
Rejoicing in her beauty, and the worship
Of the countless panting breezes, which dissolved
In extasy, commingle in her fragrance.
But sorrow is like a lily, pale and tremulous,
All glittering with the tears of early morning,
Living apart in some secluded dell,
Where veils of thickest greenery conceal
Its passing loveliness.   No poetry
Is half so dear as that which tells of sorrow.
Shakspere himself, the representative
Of all the poets of all nations, and all ages,
Never gave utterance to strains so sweet,
So soothingly delicious, as those strains
Which tell of sorrow.
Joy is the daylight when the glorious sun
Bathes earth and heaven in his radiant beauty ;
But sorrow is the moonlight, when the moon
The mystical sad moon, and all the stars

G

In loveliness unspeakable, entrance
The universe.   But night may change,
The moon may set, the stars may cease to shine,
And all will be but blackness, fearful blackness,
Which vivid lightnings only render blacker ;
But this is agony, not sorrow.

THE VISION.

A H ! well do I remember,
  In the warm month of December,
How I used to sit at even
  In a dell so very fair,
That it seemed almost like heaven,
  It was so passing fair.

A mossy bank whereon to lie
And gaze upon the fitful sky,
Grass and flowers to form a bed
With velvet cushions for my head,
While the sassafras above me
Seemed almost to love me,
They so bent their branches o'er me
  All bedeckt with starry flowers,
Raining slumb'rous odours down
  In noiseless showers.

There were mossy fern-trees near me,
  With their graceful feathered fronds,
Which they slowly waved above me,
  Like hoar magicians' wands,

Caressing the wind—till oh ! how sweet
Were the odours that fell from his wingèd feet,
Which in the heat of the noonday hours
Had brushed the scent from myriad flowers.

Shading a brook the tea-trees grew,
Spangled with blossoms of whitish hue,
Which fell from the boughs to the ground below,
As fall from heaven the flakes of snow ;
And many shrubs in the water dipped,
Flowers wide-mouthed and velvet-lipped,
Whose scented honey the ripples sipped.

There a ledge of rocks in the streamlet made
    A bright cascade,
Whose foaming waters, as they fell,
Scooped a clear refreshing well,
A deep mirror for the dell ;
For not a flower but loves to look
At its own image in the brook.

    And high above the waterfall,
In giant masses rent and riven,
Rocks clomb up almost to heaven,
    Proudly towering over all !
Except the giant gums that rose
Grand as Titans in repose :
And those tall crags were bright with many
Flowers that bloomed in every cranny,

And every clift that repeated shocks
Had torn in the heart of the caverned rocks,
While blossoms fell from the jagged eaves
In noiseless cataracts of leaves.

Ah! well do I remember
    That dell so very fair,
How in the summer even
    I used to wander there ;
And one ev'ning in December
More than all I do remember,
Towards the closing of December,
In that glen that seemed like heaven,
    It was so passing fair.

On the velvet cushions lying,
    Long I gazed with dreamy eye !
At the speckled cloudlets flying
    Through the deep unfathomed sky.

And across my soul came thronging,
    As I gazed into that sky,
Every hope and every longing
    That had ever made me sigh :
Every hope and every longing
    That had made me smile or sigh.

And in endless combinations
Came all noble aspirations,

And thoughts that knew not of control,
All—all came sweeping o'er my soul,
Like the changing clouds that sped
Through the heavens overhead.

Thus that evening was I thinking,
Now rising and now sinking,
As hope or fear would gain the best
Of the struggles in my breast,
While I pictured in my brain
   All that I might lose,
   All that I might gain,
All that man had once attained,
   All that he might attain,
All that man had once performed,
   All he might do again.

And I thought of all the hopes,
   All the glories of the strife,
Of the valleys and the mountains
   In the onward path of life ;
Till afar off in that pathway
   A mountain seemed to rise,
Which I gazed at with deep longing,
   With wondering, eager eyes.
Sometimes I was elated,
   My soul with hope upbuoyed,
Sometimes I thought 'twas fated
   All my hopes should be destroyed.

Till at last I could no more control
The heartfelt longing of my soul :
   " Is it mine," I cried, "to ponder
      'Mid its heaven of delights ?
      Can it be mine to wander
      O'er its dazzling glorious heights ? "
Scarce was the silence broken,
Scarcely had I spoken,
   When before me, in the air,
I saw a face most beautiful,
   A face so very fair,
That I thought the dell was heaven,
And the face some radiant angel
   Whose paradise was there.

Ah ! how they smiled upon me
   Those angelic radiant eyes,
   Blue and fathomless as skies,
Those glorious eyes, those more than eyes,
Those two deep souls that gazed on me,
That smiled, O God ! so heavenly.

They stayed about a breathing,
And just as I was wreathing
My fancies into words, they went,
Leaving me in dim wonderment.
They are gone, then ? Nay, not gone !
For many a night and many a morn

Has memory brought me back that smile,
Those heavenly eyes that can beguile
My spirit in its deepest sadness,
Turning sorrow into gladness,
    Turning gladness into joy.

When my soul is most despairing,
    When the hope within is dead,
And fears come stealing o'er me,
    With a stealthy night-like tread ;
And when thoughts rise up within me
    Too strong for my control,
And I cry out in the longing,
    In the anguish of my soul—
" Fool ! thinkest thou of winning
    Honour in the strife ?
Thinkest thou to climb the mountain
    In the onward path of life ?
Nay—thy path lies in the valleys,
    In the stagnant crowded alleys "—
Then that smile comes with a suddenness
    That almost makes me start,
Comes, giving back an answer
    To my doubting, feeble heart,
Giving back a glorious answer
    To the doubtings of my heart.

Ah ! ne'er shall I forget that smile
Those radiant eyes that can beguile
My spirit in its deepest sadness,
Turning sorrow into gladness,
    Turning gladness into joy.

(1855.)

THOUGHT.

THERE is ever beside me,
　　Abroad or at home,
Wherever I wander,
　　Wherever I roam,
A beautiful Spirit
　　Whose name is Thought,
Teaching me all
　　That my soul has sought.

In the depths of the Forest
　　Where tall trees rise,
Like pillars supporting
　　The dome of the skies,
Whose fathomless ether
　　Of radiant blue
Envelops the scene
　　In a rich warm hue ;

Where tremulous creepers
　　Entwine the stems
With flowers that glitter
　　And glow like gems ;

Where beautiful underwood
   Spreads around,
So thick that the sun
   Never looks on the ground—
Save through rents in the leafy roof,
   Where delicate flowers
Faint in the burning heat
   Of noonday hours.

In shady dells
   Where streamlets flow,
Merrily singing
   As they go,
And murmuring often
   Songs of love
To the boughs that droop
   From the trees above.

In mountain passes
   By earthquakes riven,
Whose clefts shut out
   The light of heaven,
Where rock upon rock
   In confusion piled,
Impart to the scene
   An aspect wild,
Where in clefts too high
   For an eagle's nest,

Some delicate flower
  Is seen to rest,
Like a calm green isle
  In a stormy sea,
Like a bright young child
  On a stern man's knee.

Like lakes that sleep
  In wooded hills,
Fed by the waters
  Of countless rills,
When over the waters
  I calmly float,
While silvery ripples
  Kiss my boat,
That sails along
  With a quiet grace,
So as not to ruffle
  The lake's still face,
Whereon the sky
  And the stars of night
Are figured and drawn
  By the soft moonlight.

By rivers that rush
  In extatic glee
In their great desire
  To reach the sea,

To mingle and mix
In the deep wild sea,
In the throbbing heart
Of their God, the sea,
Like the longing hope
Of this soul of mine,
For the beautiful truth,
For the all divine,
Like the longing of men
For the all divine.

On the craggy rocks
Of the ocean shore,
Where the breakers beat
With an angry roar ;
Where the ripples run
On the sandy beach,
With the mystic sound
Of an unknown speech,
With a measured fall
And a music of rhyme,
Like one of the songs
Of the olden time.

And when to the shore
The ocean brings
For his bride, the earth,
All beautiful things,

Shells and pearls
　And soft seaweeds,
Sponges and mosses,
　And coral beads.
On the foaming ocean,
　That restless soul,
Condemned for ever
　To heave and roll ;
To struggle for ever,
　Yet never gain,
To strive for ever,
　Yet strive in vain.

And far from the ocean
　And forest dell,
In populous cities
　Where thousands dwell,
In the streets incessantly
　To and fro,
Wide human rivers
　That come and go—
Where virtue and vice
　Are in one band,
Where love and hate
　Go hand in hand,
There and wherever
　I wander or roam,

In the forest shade
  On the ocean foam,
In the noisy town,
  In the quiet home,
There is by me a spirit
  Whose name is Thought,
Teaching me all
  That my soul has sought.

(*Dec.* 1855.)

ANNIE.

———

I AM lonely, oh, my Annie!
　　Very lonely without thee!
And my soul is full of longing
　　For that I may not see!
Of longing inexpressible,
　　For that which cannot be.

Where art thou, oh, my Annie?
　　Is thy spirit near me now?
Are these thy spirit-kisses
　　That I feel upon my brow?
Or is it but a wind that comes
　　Upblowing from the sea,
From the shore whereon so often
　　I have wandered, Love, with thee?

Tell me, what is this wild singing,
　　This sweet music that I hear?
Are they not thy spirit-whispers,
　　Breathing low into mine ear?

Or are they but a music
  Wafted upward from the sea?
Are they but the mystic music
  Of the pensive she-oak tree—
But the voices of the she-oak
  That are singing, Love, of thee?

Ah! when I think, my Annie,
  Of the days that are gone by,
When I brood in starless silence,
  Broken only by the sigh
Sadly breathed for those bright hours
  In the days that are gone by,
Oh, my Annie! I am lonely—
  Very lonely without thee,
And my soul is full of longing
  For that which cannot be.

More than ever am I lonely
  When I wander by the sea,
For its rolling and its heaving
  Bring sad memories of thee—
Of those sweet summer evenings
  When we two were wont to stroll,
And watch in deepest silence
  The waves enchanted roll:
In silence that was eloquent,
  The converse of the soul.

H

And I think of how we listened
  To the music of the sea,
When to my fancy not a wave
  But sang a song of thee.
I think of how we loved to sit
  And watch the ripples beat
Upon the sand, as though they strove
  To reach to our rocky seat,
As though they did quite long to print
  Their kisses on thy feet.

So am I not most lonely,
  Oh, my Annie ! without thee?
And alas ! it is not only
  When I wander by the sea.
For even in the forest
  Not a shrub and not a tree,
Not the tiniest, poorest flower
  But it speaks to me of thee.

For I think of how we wandered
  By the laughing joyous river,
Saw the scented tea-tree branches
  Which for very joy did quiver,
As they dipt them in its waters,
  As they mingled in the river.

How we saw the spreading myrtles,
 Saw the cypress and the vine,
Saw the green festoons and bowers
 Of the dark macquarie vine,
Saw the blackwoods and the boxtrees.
 And the spiral sassafrases,
Saw the fairy fern trees mantled
 With their mossy cloak of grasses.

Now we saw the gum-tree rising
 Very far above the rest,
Saw in its topmost branches
 The wailing magpies' nest,
Heard the mimi chatter, chatter,
 Saw the bright rosellas fly,
With breasts that glowed like sunsets
 In the fiery western sky;
Saw the cockatoo above us,
 Heard its wild unearthly scream,
And saw the deep blue kingfisher
 Dart swiftly o'er the stream.

So not a bird or flower
 But speaks to me of thee,
Not a tree within the forest,
 Not a wave upon the sea,
Not a ripple on the river
 But whispers, Love, of thee.

And oh ! I feel so wretched
   When I'm sitting in my room,
That once was bright and sunny,
   Though now it is all gloom ;
I take the books I loved so well,
   But oh ! it is in vain,
When the words are only words,
   Not thoughts within the brain :
Not thoughts as they were wont to be,
   Not pictures in the brain.

All their stores of wit and humour
   Give a deeper shade to grief,
All my learning, all my studies
   Can give me no relief ;
And all sad tales of sorrow
   Make me feel still more alone ;
For, thinking upon others' grief,
   I think upon my own.
So I am lonely, Annie,
   Very lonely without thee,
And my soul is full of longing
   For that which cannot be.

Oh, my Annie ! I am weary,
   Very weary of the strife,
In this bitter anxious loneliness,
   This desert land of life,

That sets me thinking, asking,
    What is death, and what is life ;
What is truth, and what is falsehood,
    Are they really what they seem ?
Or, are they mere illusions—
    But a dim and empty dream ?

For are we not eternal ?
    Is not this, that we call life,
A sleep of the eternal soul,
    A transient dream of strife,
And death a mere awakening
    To the grand eternal life ?
And all our thoughts of holiness,
    Of beauty and of love,
Oh ! are they not deep memories
    Of our former life above ?
Come and tell me, oh, my Annie !
    Tell me if those things be true,
Tell me if I shall awaken
    Back again to life with you ?

Thou not long ago awakened,
    Thou hast risen from thy sleep,
And wilt surely come from heaven,
    Thou wilt surely come and keep
A gentle watching o'er me,
    Till I also wake from sleep.

For I am lonely, Annie,
Very lonely, without thee,
And my soul is full of longing
For that which may not be :
Full of longing inexpressible,
To live and be with thee.

(*Dec.* 1855.)

THE OLD AND THE NEW YEAR.

Dec. 29, 1855.

NONE shed a tear
   For the poor old year,
Though the poor old year is going to die ;
   None shed a tear,
   None heave a sigh,
No one cares if he live or die.

The poor old year, the dying year,
No one wails and no one grieves,
Though some kind hand has strewn his bier
With a covering of green leaves ;
Besprinkled o'er with choicest flowers,
As memories of the wingèd hours,
The old year's babes, the flitting hours.

   The poor old year,
   Away he goes,
   With all his joys,
   And all his woes ;

Yet no cloud to dim the skies,
No tear in night's deep mystic eyes,
    No funeral gales,
    No wind that wails,
    No mournful tones,
    No tree that sighs,
    No stream that moans,
No one weeping, no one sighing,
Though the poor old year is dying.

Will no one weep a tear of sorrow
For the year that dies to-night ?
Oh no ! the new year comes to-morrow ;
All are dreaming with delight
Of the long expected comer,
The dear darling of the summer.
Oh no ! we cannot shed a tear
Though he be dying, poor old year !

For half in hope, and half in fear,
Think we of the bright new year,
Who with the hours will come down
At the twinkling of the morrow ;
On his head a magic crown,
A crown of mingled joy and sorrow.
So give him then a joyous meeting,
Give him a right hearty greeting ;

Welcome him with joy and gladness,
So his crown may lose its sadness,
While the joy may still be there,
Raining blessings everywhere.
Oh ! should we hope, or should we fear,
The coming of the glad new year?

The poor old year !
On his leafy bier
Lies the dying year ;
And even now methinks I hear
The coming of the far-off year ;
Yes, I surely hear his coming,
Hear the rustling of his coming,
    Nearer and more near ;
Hear the musical low humming
    Of the hours that throng the year ;
And methinks I hear a breathing
    From the flowers,
See their balmy incense wreathing
    In sweet showers,
See the lofty tree-tops swinging
    In submission to the year ;
Hear the soft wind singing
    Praises in his ear,
See the stars in heaven above
Smiling in their quiet love.

But what is it makes the moon so pale?
What is it makes the moon so white?
Doth she weep or doth she wail
For the poor old year, who dies to-night?
Oh no! she doth not weep nor wail:
'Tis passion that makes the moon so pale,
'Tis passionate love for the bright new year;
Not sorrow for the year who dies,
Not sorrow for the year who lies
Forgotten on his leafy bier.
Oh no! she doth not weep nor wail,
'Tis passion makes the moon so pale:
Passion for the glad new comer,
The bright darling of the radiant summer.

  Then banish sorrow,
  Banish sadness,
  Be all joy,
  And be all gladness;
Shed no tear and heave no sigh,
Let laughter lurk in every eye,
Set a crown of joy on every brow,
For the glad new year is coming now.
So sing the song and ring the cheer,
He comes! he comes! the glad new year.

BELATED.

"A H ! my poor wife will be anxious
   At my coming home so late,
And my children now are waiting
   For me, at the garden gate.

" For fast the day is dying ;
   There is scarcely any light,
And darker still and darker,
   Grow the dreary shades of night.

" Like dusky phantoms round me
   The peppermints arise ;
And the wind among their branches,
   How it sobs and how it sighs !

" And the bark goes tatter, tatter,
   As it beats against the tree,
Oh ! would to God it were not dark,
   So that I might but see—

" If it only is the clatter
   Of the bark against the tree,
And not the stealthy patter
   Of some horrid thing by me.

" Hark ! I hear a fearful hissing,
   Low and loathsome, as I pass,
From the dry ferns and the rushes,
   From the tussocks of rank grass.

" Oh ! how it makes me tremble,
   Walking through this dismal brake,
For the very step I'm treading now
   May fall upon a snake.

" What is that in the path before me,
   Like a spectre dim and gaunt ?
This must be some demon prison,
   This must be some goblin haunt !

" Tush ! I rave : it is no spectre,
   It is only a dead tree ;
'Tis passing strange, that ghostly things
   Like these should master me.

" And what is this wild sound I hear,
   Strikes terror to my mind ?
It is but the branches howling,
   As they wrestle in the wind.

" And what is this loud screaming,
   To my heart sounds like a knell ?
My God ! it is the black men's cry,
   Their fiendish, savage yell."

So spake a wayworn traveller,
　And as he spoke he fell ;
For the war-cry of the black men
　Was indeed his funeral knell.

True were all his sad misgivings,
　True were all his ghostly fears ;
For there he died in the forest,
　Slain by the quivering spears
Of the blacks, who will dance their dances,
　In their wild and savage glee,
Dance in the glowing firelight,
　The wild corrobery.

All this while the little children
　Stood at the garden gate,
Saying, " Oh, we wonder what can keep him ?
　What can make our father late ? "
They looked into the forest,
　But could see nothing there,
Save the waving ghostly branches,
　Making moanings in the air.

Then they stand awhile in silence,
　Put their ear upon the ground,
In hopes to catch the lightest noise,
　To hear the faintest sound,
That seemed at all like footsteps,
　As they fell upon the ground.

And they heard the moaning branches,
   And the rustling of the air ;
They heard the wild cat screaming
   As he sprang from out his lair ;
And they heard the brown opossums,
   As they leapt from tree to tree ;
Heard all these—but not the footsteps
   Of him they longed to see.

Sat all night the mother watching,
   With a brow that ached with care ;
She looked into the darkness,
   And gazed into the air ;
And at the fire, as if she hoped
   To find some comfort there ;
And when her husband comes not,
   Comes not morrow after morrow,
Oh ! who shall tell her wretchedness,
   Her agony of sorrow !

(1855.)

THE SUMMONS.

———

" WHERE are you going to-night, my child?"
    "To the forest, father."
    "What! are you wild,
To think of going to the forest to-night?
Why, girl! you would almost die with fright,
Alone in the forest, this darksome night!"
"Nay, hear you not in the air around,
Hear you not, father, the weird-like sound
Of angels' wings and the music sweet,
The gentle patter of spirit-feet?
And hear you not what these angels say?
They call me, my father: I cannot stay;
The angels call me, I must away.
And hear you not, father, from every tree,
The forest demons calling me?
Oh! do you not hear them chiding me,
For talking, father, so long with thee?
Farewell! farewell! I must begone;
They mock me that I tarry so long."
"Good God! My girl, you are out of your mind!
The demons you hear are only the wind,

As it howls and mutters amid the trees.
How is it that these fantasies,
These silly thoughts, have so filled your brain,
That you cannot hear the wind or rain,
But you must fancy that angels call? "
" Oh ! see you not yon phantoms tall,
Crowding in a ghostly band,
How each one waves a shadowy hand,
Beckoning me to their spirit-land ?
Farewell ! farewell ! I must not stay ;
They call me, my father : I must away ! "

And into the darkness, the wind and the rain,
She flew, and she never was seen again.

THE RACE.

PART I.

1.

M Y soul is full of gladness,
With never a tinge of sadness ;
For joy is life, and life is joy,
And I feel all life, and every breath
Has a spell in its freshness to ward off death.

2.

Surely I am all immortal,
And the grave's dim portal
     Never can close on me :
And this blessed air that we have for nought
Is the magic draught that was vainly sought,
With infinite toil by the baffled sages,
The alchemists of the middle ages :
Aye ! this is the essence that doth inspire,
This is the true Promethean fire.

3.

My horse feels the same wild joy as I,
He seems as though he could never die,

And I feel beneath me his tremulous bound,
As though he scarce deigned to put foot on the ground:
But I curb him in, to bask awhile
In the rosy beauty of morn's young smile.

4.

All things are joyous; the very earth
Pants in an atmosphere of mirth,
And her warm breath rises to morn above,
Freighted with worship and joy and love;
While from the flowers that grow around
Comes a murmured thrilling sound,
Felt, not heard, like a spirit's voice
That comes in our sorrow to bid us rejoice.

5.

See the river, how it rushes!
Hear how merrily it gushes!
As if it did rejoice
In music like the voice
Of merry children at their play,
In the close of some sweet summer day.

6.

Watch the ripples swiftly dancing
        As they run,
Every moment slyly glancing
        At the sun,

Who peeps at them through the jealous myrtles,
Which cover the stream with their dark green kirtles.

7.

All things are glad ; not a blade of glass
But nods as the laughing breezes pass :
And the sweet musk flowers are pale with delight,
And the blackwood tall, and the sassafras
Burn and glow in emerald light,
For not a leaf but has a gem
Plucked from Aurora's diadem.

8.

Aye, all rejoice, save the gums alone,
Who are far too proud to laugh or moan,
Caring not to borrow
From others' gladness joy or sorrow ;
For all the elements conspire
To make them proud: the forest fire
On them is impotent—the wildest storm
But makes them music. So they stand
Silent ever, still and grand,
Full of their own great glory
Like the angel of the story,
Who grew so great, he thought that God
Must bow and tremble at his nod.

9.

Yet I know an axe that would ring them all,
Though even then they would not fall,
But after death would still arise
Majestically to the skies,
Like a memory of the good and wise.

10.

But who is it yonder, that rides so fast,
Like a swallow borne on by the boisterous blast?
'Tis surely some lady, the skirts of her dress
     Are streaming behind,
And the many folds of her beautiful tress,
     All unconfined,
Float on the waves of the odorous wind.

11.

How bright she is! how very fair!
Can it be Jessie? ah, would that it were!
But her home is much too far away
For her to be here by break of day.
Besides, the pony she rides is white
As a cockatoo in its onward flight,
But this one before me is black as night.
But come, my steed, and let us try
Our best to solve the mystery.

12.

I let the rein fall on his arching neck,
And away he flew without let or check,
            Away, away, away!
Like a ball from the gun,
Like a ray from the sun,
            Away, away, away!
Flinging the dust, and the grass and the flowers,
Far behind us in motley showers.

13.

Away! away! we leap with ease
All the hollows and fallen trees,
Thundering over the stones and rocks,
Which sometimes give us terrible shocks
But they matter not, for I only think
To overtake at the river's brink
This mystic beautiful being who seems
Bright as the queen of our longing dreams.

14.

She surely will stop at the river's brink;
It is far too wide for the horse to leap:
Besides, the bank is terribly steep,
The current swift and the waters deep.

15.

Good God ! is she mad ? in—in she dashes ;
Above and around her the water splashes,
Above and around her the water flashes,
While the drops, ere they fall in the river's bed,
Form a shrine o'er her nymph-like head.

16.

We are both in the river, and every bound
Scatters the water in showers around.
Hurrah ! hurrah ! another bound,
Another, and we too shall ride
Both together, side by side.

17.

What, Jessie ? Yes, 'twas Jessie only
    Who had given me this chase,
Though I half thought ' twas some spirit,
    Till I saw her laughing face.

18.

All that morn across the heather
We galloped joyously together,
Yet scarcely spoke we to each other,
Though each one of the other thought ;
Or, if we spoke at all, ' twas only
Just a few words said in sport.

19.

That was indeed a joyous ride,
As we galloped side by side,
Each thinking what the other thought,
Each seeking what the other sought :
Like two laughing rivers rushing,
Like two joyous rivers brushing
Odours from the flowers and grass,
Over which their breathings pass
Ere they mingle into one ;
So our very souls became
Absorbed and mingled in the same.

20.

Together gazed we at the sun,
Together gazed into the sky,
On the clouds that flitted by,
And at the mists which seemed to rise,
Ethereal spirits to the skies,
Unwillingly from their sweet rest
In the dark blue mountain's breast.
Like the tales that legends old
To our charmèd ears unfold,
How angels left their home above
To taste the joys of earthly love,
And how, when they must needs arise
Back again to Paradise,

They gave to those they left behind
The beauty of ethereal mind.
And so those mountains seemed to me
To have become more heavenly,
From mingling with the mists that rose
Slowly—slowly—from repose.

21.

We gazed upon the waving plain,
With its fringe of wooded hills ;
Saw the gushing, laughing river,
Heard the music of its rills.
Then looked once more upon the mountain,
The birthplace of its bubbling fountain ;
Still more into the deep blue skies,
And then into each other's eyes.

22.

And as across the ocean
Come the waves with onward roll,
Waves of passionate emotion
Came crowding o'er my soul :
And words of fervent meaning
Fell swiftly from my tongue,
Words as passionate as those
That burning Sappho sung.

Every passionate desire,
Every wild and longing thought,
On the anvil of my passions
Into shape and meaning wrought.
Unto one that joyed to hear,
All I did impart;
I spoke the fervent passion,
All the deep love of my heart.

———

PART II.

1.

IN a rambling long verandah,
  A month or so thereafter,
What sounds there were of merriment,
  Of chattering and laughter,
Of shouts and songs that shook the dust
  From many a trembling rafter.

2.

The pattering of tiny feet,
Little satin lovelinesses,
Peeping in and out the dresses,
Dancing to the music sweet,
As up above, the starry crowds
Peep in and out the mantling clouds;

The soft low hum of whispered speeches,
Of the love that Cupid teaches;
Music, laughter, dancing, singing,
Were the sounds so gladly ringing,
Ringing through the midnight air,
Awakening echoes everywhere.

3.

And there were many beaming glances,
Swift and soft as moonlight fancies,
Blushing cheeks and beating hearts,
Odd surprises, pretty starts,
Many unexpected meetings,
Hearty welcome, joyous greetings,
Many jests and idle vows,
Winks and smiles, and nods and bows,
And hands a little warmly prest,
And thrills through many a fair one's breast.

4.

And up and down the garden walks
Were shady strolls and quiet talks,
And, as no doubt the flowers know,
Now and then a kiss or so;
And now and then an arm embraced
Of course, a most unwilling waist.

5.

Well, then came supper after all,
The crown and climax of the ball;
And there was one old wheezy uncle
Grew so affable that night,
That every red carbuncle
Seemed just bursting with delight;
And when he'd coughed and blown his nose,
He told us that he now arose,
Intending to congratulate
His worthy friend upon the late
Auspicious union of his son—
You know the rest: for everyone
Makes the same speech on such occasions,
Venturing on no innovations;
And he spoke till he could speak no more,
And then sat down amid a roar
Of voices—in uproarious glee,
"The bride and bridegroom," three times three!

(1855.)

LOVE IN HATE.

I PASS you by as cold as death,
With never a frown, and never a smile,
Though I love you dearly all the while,
Love and hate you all in a breath.

Though I hate you so I could kill you, Love !
Kill you and watch you as you die,
With scorn on my lip and joy in my eye,
Yet I love you intensely still, Love !

For excess of hate will turn to love,
And excess of love delights in hate ;
And so for ever I oscillate
From love to hate, and from hate to love.

I never try to forget you, Love !
But think of you oft for your own dear sake,
And all that has passed can never make
Me curse the day when I met you, Love !

' Tis vain to bewail, vain to regret,
Better I knew you than knew you not ;
Nay, even if pain were my constant lot,
I would bless the day we two first met.

And you ? I know you must think of me yet
With intensity that can never abate,
Perchance in love, perchance in hate,
But whichever it be, you can never forget.

Forget ! ah no ! we can never smother,
Or weep away in a few light tears,
A love that lasted for many years,
So we must both love and hate each other.

Things have passed of so black a dye
As to embitter our mutual life,
To kindle a passive yet deadly strife
Which never shall lose its intensity.

And I hate you so, if you prayed me now,
I would add a pang to your agony ;
And I hope you would do the same for me,
With a smile of scorn on your beautiful brow.

For our strife may never end, unless
We lose our memories with our breath,
And lie asleep in the lap of death,
Drunk with the stream of forgetfulness.

Let us pray to God that it may be so :
And yet I beseech you never abate
One atom of love, one atom of hate,
Let us love and hate though, whether or no.

Let us pray to God in heaven above,
That forgetting the past, we may rise at length,
Twin souls in new-born glory and strength,
To a mutual world of life and love.

(*Feb.* 1856.)

SELF IN NATURE, NATURE IN SELF.

W HAT are the uses of Nature, I ask,
    Of hills and valleys, of woods and streams ?
Are they only made that man may bask
    In the languid light of aimless dreams ?

Are they made that man may dream away
    A life that is fitted for nobler things ?
May rest content with the fancies' play
    On the poor light thoughts that Nature brings ?

We are made to mix in the common strife
    For noble deeds, for glorious ends ;
And to think that a life of dreams is life,
    Is a shallow cheat the Devil sends.

Must we contemplate a half-dead life,
    A life that is far beyond our own,
Before we can rise to the Infinite life,
    To the mighty All—to the One alone ?

From Nature to God we hope to rise :
    Tush ! it is but an idle task ;
We see ourselves in a new disguise,
    We worship self in a double mask.

Or say we climb the ladder of thought
   To thoughts of heaven from thoughts of earth,
So the battle of life remain unfought,
   Our clearest thoughts are nothing worth.

Why must the poet for ever sing
   Nature's glories of woods and streams?
Why soars he not on a stronger wing,
   To higher aims, to greater themes?

In the love and hate of the human heart,
   In its hopes and fears, its joys and woes,
There is more, far more than hath a part
   In all the beauties Nature shows.

There is more, I say, in one man's heart,
   In one man's soul that breathes and lives,
More for the poet's and painter's art,
   Than in all the thoughts that Nature gives.

Though the poet and painter, I must confess,
   Give Nature a beauty besides her own,
They picture her native loveliness,
   And add the feeling, impart the tone.

For Nature is as an empty flask,
   And their souls run in like precious wine,
They wrap themselves in a leafy mask,
   They place themselves in a leafy shrine.

And though I myself love Nature well,
'Tis not with a superstitious love ;
I deem her not as some would tell
    The expression here of a God above.

Why do I love yon mountain there,
    With its wrinkled brow, and glory of snow ?
Why do I ever gaze up there,
    With scarce a thought of the plain below ?

Oh ! the sight of its form, and beauty of blue
    Recalls a memory of one
With eyes of a deeper and holier hue,
    And hair like the rays of a golden sun.

Once I recollect when the mountain's form
    Loomed like a ghost through its sheet of cloud,
When the hills grew dark at the voice of the storm,
    And the forests quivered aloud, aloud.

We two were standing on yonder knoll,
    And she was watching tremblingly ;
But the storm and I became one soul,
    I in it, and it in me.

And the love there is in the hearts of men
    Lies at rest in its purple bowl,
Till something comes as the storm came then,
    And wakes the passion of all the soul.

K

And I clasped her then as the storm clasped me,
  In a torrent of passion, of hopes and fears,
While she half drew back, half nestled to me,
  Then trembled away in a heaven of tears.

Oh ! the world in love, the life in love,
  Life and love are surely one ;
There can be no life without a love,
  There cannot be day if there be no sun.

Though I should live for a thousand years,
  Each hour crowned with a rose of delight,
I know full well I should find no peers,
  To that one hour of that wild night.

Though all my life had been one storm
  Of misery, of sorrow, and pain,
For the fulness and bliss of that one hour
  I would live it all—all over again.

No wonder then, that I love so well
  To gaze on that hoary mountain brow,
For the love of that night has a mighty spell,
  A power to move me even now.

Though Nature, as it seems to me,
  Has a higher use than to be but ripe
With remembrances like a history
  Of man's, or even a nation's life ;

Nature, I say, has a higher use,
  Although it is apt to degenerate
To lower ends, to a mean abuse,
  To a shallow love, or a shallower hate.

But I hold it to be a mirror of self,
  Where we may see the outs and ins,
Not alone of the soul that bows to pelf,
  Not alone of self that errs and sins.

For in it our higher self appears,
  The soul as cleansed from taint of earth,
With all the gathered strength of years,
  And the pristine purities of birth.

Let us think on self as we view it there,
  How far we may rise, how far we may fall,
But oh! as we gaze, beware! beware!
  Lest we worship self for the one and all!

  (*March* 1856.)

MY LOVE.

OH ! she is fair, this Love of mine,
    With golden hair, and eyes of blue ;
So dewy soft and crystalline,
Eyes that I can look into ;
And as I look can well divine
The world of passionate love that lies
In the slumb'rous depths of those tremulous eyes

Her brow is just a trifle high,
But rising like a pillar of snow
From a cluster of crimson flowers,
From her cheeks which are all aglow,
With the blushes that come and go,
As I talk with her in the evening hours,
All alone with her and the flowers.

And her voice it is so soft and sweet,
Like a summer wind in its rise and fall,
Like a soul that is audible ;
The words seem scarcely words at all,
But thoughts that are made musical,
And I listen chained in their silver spell,
As the angels listen to Israfel.

Oh ! I love her for this beauty of hers,
For her love so pure, and her heart so true,
And for a thousand other things,
Which, should I tell them now to you,
Would seem so small, unless you knew
As I know, all the secret springs,
Of these seemingly little things.

I take her face, that dear young face,
With my two hands I take it so,
I part her golden tresses back,
Like sunbeams from her brow of snow ;
And I kiss with lips that burn and glow,
Her dear, dear lips, that quiver and tremble
With the passion they would dissemble.

The passion that makes me feel more strong,
Makes her restless as the light ;
Her love is an agony of fears,
And pain is so mingled with her delight,
That oftener she bursts into tears,
And with a passionate sense of unrest
Her tears and blushes are hid in my breast.

   (*August* 1856.)

THE POET SOUL.

A S an islet amid islands
Is the world amid the stars,
And a grand eternal ocean
Is without its narrow bars ;
And we may see this ocean
Surging up these isles of time,
May hear its spaceless music
Hymning thoughts and things sublime.

Though time and space surround us
Grimly everywhere we turn,
And would hide this mighty beauty
Of the spaceless and eterne ;
Yet there is that within us
Time and space cannot control :
Would you know it, O my brother ?
'Tis the faithful poet-soul.

Oh ! this world is dull and dreary,
So we often blindly say,
When some evil shadow haunts us,
Growing deeper day by day ;

But the blackest night of evil,
   And the wildest seas of crime,
Are all bounded by the circle
   Of those shadows, space and time.
And we all may rise above them
   To the glorious light of day,
While the evil dreams that haunt us
   Shall like phantoms pass away.
For there is that can wing us
   Where the world has no control :
Would you know it, O my brother ?
   'Tis the faithful poet-soul.

Would you look on sin and sorrow
   Through the golden light of love ?
Would you in life's blackest moments
   Keep the heavens still blue above ?
Would you learn what wond'rous magic
   Gives us all the power to trace
Undreamt eternal beauties
   In things ne'er so foul and base ?
Would you see in all things round us,
   Be they great or be they small,
Something truer, something higher,
   Would you see the God in all ?
There is a power within us,
   Has all this in its control :
Would you know it, O my brother?
   'Tis the faithful poet-soul.

PRAYER.

———

WHAT are these that we call prayers?
　　Are they drawling words we mutter,
With pious twang and upturned eyes,
Or voiceless things, too deep to utter,
Given in sobs and passionate cries?
What are these and what are prayers?

Words are very seldom prayers:
Mere prayer-echoes—scarcely more—
Of the deep things of the heart,
Struggling at the inmost core
Of our beings; thus they start
Into life and into prayer.

All we do is but a prayer :
All we think and all we feel,
Brings us either joy or woe,
As it makes its mute appeal
To heaven above, or hell below,
For there is no unanswered prayer.
All life is but an actual prayer,
And most unregarded things,

So they are of faith and love,
Bear us, as on angels' wings,
To the throne of God above :
For a life of love is God's own prayer.

(20th January, 1857.)

LONGING—YEARNING.

———•———

WAS there ever earnest soul,
  Struggling bravely to its goal,
But that felt amidst the throng
Of its longings right and wrong,
None so fervent, none so strong,
As the longing of its being for a voice?

 Was there ever man who sought,
 Ever man who thought a thought,
But his most intense desire,
All absorbing, all entire,
Burning in his heart like fire,
Was the longing for his thought to find a voice?

 In the golden dreams of youth,
 In the eager search for truth,
In the feverish knowledge thirst,
In the passions wildly nurst,
 Till the heart doth almost burst,
There is evermore a yearning for a voice.

Whatsoever be our fate,
Do we love, or do we hate,
Have we hope to do and dare,
Or if wearied out with care,
Lie we buried in despair,
Still our souls are ever yearning for a voice.

Thought itself is but a speech
Of things words can never reach,
But which dimly seen at best,
Striving still to be expressed,
Never let the soul have rest,
So intensely burns their longing for a voice.

This one wish belongs to all,
Be we ne'er so great or small,
In our mighty spirit strife,
With this hope our hearts are rife,
With the longing of all life,
For the burning soul within to find a voice.

(*January* 1857.)

THE POET ARTISAN.

THIS world of ours is blind to its own good,
    And beauty dwells where least we look for it.
We search the uttermost earth with eagerness
For some small flower we set our hearts upon.
And when all hopes of finding it are dead,
We see it blossoming at our very doors.
Streams that might wash whole valleys into plenty,
And clasp the sunlight in their waves of blue,
Are sobbing to themselves beneath our feet,
Tumultuously welling in dark caves,
And yearning to leap forth into the light.
So the world's great ones, who might conquer death,
Are linked to common things that clog their strength
And weigh them still to earth. Though nought so
    small
But gains a hallowed beauty at their touch,
And gathers grandeur from their nobleness.
For these impress their individual mark
On every thing. I once knew such an one,
With pale sad face, and ample breadth of brow,
And passionate blue veins that throbbed and pulsed

Tumultuously, when aught had movèd him ;
And compressed lips that spoke no wavering,
But something sought, and found not : not despaired of,
But still sought.   Two large deep eyes,
Which ever seemed to gaze on things afar,
To have dim glimmerings into mystery,
And pierce the threshold of the weird unknown ;
Eyes luminously dark, wherein we felt
His noblest being was concèntrated.
His frame was weakly ; slender at the first ;
Grown slenderer with long ill-requited toil,
Though his thin arms were moved with fiery strength,
And stubborn iron parted with such blows
As you would think would almost shatter him.
For years he worked the dull monotonous round,
From earliest morning far into the night,
In a long room where was the ceaseless din
Of straps and wheels and mad machinery—
And shrill set sounds that clave the heavy air,
The dead stale air, rank with poisonous breath
Breathed and re-breathed into a sickly stench,
So dull and dark too, with a grimy dust,
That the red sun scarce dared to look at them,
Save with a yellow glow of feverish light
That was no light—

                        But he scarce noticed it---
For men grow used to this, a most sad use.

'Twere better that we could not, but 'tis so ;
Bodies and souls alike, nothing so bad,
But half its badness ceases with long use.
And years' experience taught his hands to work
With swift mechanic motion, cleaving out
The clamorous metal into accurate lines.
His soul the while cleaving the circling lines
That pass from thought to realms where thought is
    not,
That bridge the viewless with the visible world.
Forsooth, the way that led him through the world
Was not smooth, nor carpeted with ease,
With festooned flowers carefully shutting out
Some ugly sight beyond ; but bristling stones,
And gaping clefts, danger on every side.
The devious track is the open plain of the world,
With a few flowers, say, glimmering here and there,
In nooks and corners and dim crevices,
Which he would treasure up most lovingly
As messages from heaven.

            For all stray hours,
All odd ten minutes and the one day of rest,
Which his companions chiefly spent in bed,
In a half-doze with Sunday newspapers
And plentiful libations of bad beer,
He spent in reading with his earnest eyes,
Pressing the innermost meaning from his books ;

Till brightest dreams of poet were his own,
And noblest hopes incorporate with him,
And thoughts long wand'ring through the unconscious
    world
Scarce recognised, would touch his answ'ring soul,
Take root, and kindle in impetuous life.
And Art he loved too, with a passionate love,
Seemed almost worship. I have seen him sit
And stare his soul out at some pictured form,
Although mere painted canvas, with sweet eyes
And marvellous small hands ; but giving him
Deep glimpses of unspoken loveliness
Of worlds of beauty near and yet afar,
Where heaven and earth show linked in harmony ;
And doting thus on Art and on his books,
There suddenly came a wish into his heart,
To see the land where Art and Poetry
Were living presences—Shakspere's self, he said,
The Englishest of poets, loved to weave
Old Roman story with strong English song ;
And half our paintings now but echo back
Some grand creation of grand Italy.
This wish, at first a mere wish, grew and grew
Into intensest longing, that merged all
The lesser yearnings, till his whole soul burned,
But with this only—this the only aim
For which he toiled—to gaze on Italy.
No very heroic aim, you say, and rightly too.

'Twas but a poor weak aim, yet still an aim,
And that is something in our frittered lives.
Nor was it strange that one who had lived his life
In the great city, 'mid the smoke and soot,
'Mid long black walls, and flat white window rows,
In drear succession, lengthening down the street—
It was not strange, I think, that one who had lived
With no more knowledge of the free green earth
Than market gardens, or suburban fields,
Tea-garden architecture, ruins done to death,
Set in the foreground with a tree or two
That draggled out their piteous death in life,
The ghostly city in the distant view—
Its spires and chimneys telling through the mist
Confusedly, as in a troubled dream—
It was not strange for one who had so lived,
To long for an utter change—to yearn
For a land where Art and Nature, hand in hand,
Working together with the selfsame aim,
Have reared a canonisèd loveliness.
Perchance he thought too, that a sudden touch
Of inspiration, flooding heart and brain,
Would raise him to the level of those men
Whose ashes have made Italy consecrate.
Perchance expecting a new sense of God,
A visible presence acting everywhere,
From the motionless sun to the lightest leaf that stirs
On summer winds that imperceptibly

Shoot through the air. Not knowing that God dwells
In th' expressionless face of the withered crone who
   sits
At the street-corner, crying with cracked voice,
In ceaseless monotone, her meagre wares,
More plainly than in bluest of blue skies :
Not knowing, if we cannot feel God's hand
In the smoky city, we can never see
His power elsewhere ; but a mockery only,
Our own souls playing at God—no more.
However, right or wrong, this dream possessed him,
The creaking pivot of a shattered life ;
For this he toiled, deprived himself of rest
And all those household comforts that man has
To call a home ; though, truth to tell, he had
A most rare knack of giving meanest things
An air of beauty—almost a woman's power
Of transfiguring poverty : so his room,
With its one chair, one box that was at once
Table and wardrobe, with its white window blind,
And its one blood-red geranium blossoming up
From circlets of green leaves, seemed paradise
Amid the reeking filth and sights and sounds
That made the street show like a loathsome ditch.
But this incessant toil and fever-fret
Seemed wearing out his life, until he grew
Thus pale and thin, with blue veins standing out
With death-like clearness on his pallid brow,   .

L

All withering slowly, save his luminous eyes,
Which still dilated into fitful light.
His cheeks too, wasted as they were and wan,
Were over flushed with blushes like a girl's,
As clouds rose-tinted at the death of day.

Upon a railway platform, one pure night,
I met him for the last time : he had ceased
His toil for ever—and the impatient train
That was to realise his life-long dream,
Audibly panting, with wild blood-shot eyes,
Stood yearning to plunge forth into the night,
Impetuous rushing as in demon chase.
So I had scarcely time to say " Good bye !"
When the wild whistle sounded, and he fled
To Italy—

        There as the sun sank down
In a calm sky of blue, he gazed on Rome,
And sudden joy flushed up into his face,
Too passionately for his shattered frame ;
And so, with Rome still glowing in his eyes,
With Roman music throbbing in his ears,
With " Rome " just dying on his trembling lips,
The one dream of his life expressed—he died.

(January 1857.)

THE JOURNEY.

THE day is hot as day can be,
Too hot to read, too hot to think,
The grasshoppers leave off their pranks ;
Nay, the very flies begin to see
They'd be better at rest than bothering me :
And as I lie on the river brink,
And watch its flowing like a dream,
Can only wish I were changed to a stream
Dawdling on mid shady banks,
Making love to the prettiest flowers,
Just to while away the lazy hours.

Earth is one blissful dream of ease ;
The very winds can only keep
A drowsy buzzing 'mid the trees,
Or kiss the flowers and fall asleep ;
While I keep watching, with half-shut eye,
Bright insects flitting dreamily by,
And birds above in the gorgeous sky.

And not a ripple on the stream,
And not a tremble of the breeze,

But brings to me its own sweet dream.
And visions come floating in airy clouds,
Merrily down on each golden gleam
Of sunshine glimmering 'mid the trees ;
And all I see begins to change
Into fantasies as wild and strange
As visions of sleep, but far more true ;
Nay, this very world seems but a dream,
And I a dream float on a dream,
With a gorgeous host of tinted clouds,
Through the glowing calm of the radiant blue.

But all my visions vanish in air,
It is nearly time for the train to go ;
It is striking six by this mouldy clock,
There in the turret, that seems to mock
The sexton bearded, bald and bare ;
With the windows twain and niches between,
And stiff old ivy-bushes below,
Like a grisly beard dyed black and green.

It is hard, on a burning day like this,
To rush away from my dreamy bliss,
To a sort of suicidal slaughter ;
But a train has no heart: what must be must,
Though the road is like a river of dust

And I am no more flesh and blood,
But, oozing away in dirty water,
Shall change at last to a pool of mud.

There stands the train, just ready to go,
The people swarming to and fro,
While the station-master is ringing his bell.
And the engine gives a horrible yell,
Rising out of a cloud of steam,
Like a fiery shout in a fiery dream—
A rush, a grasp, and puffing and blowing,
I open a door as the train is going,
Leaving the porter scolding and swearing,
As if one soul in the world was caring ;
I cram myself into my place,
Recover my breath and wipe my face,
And find myself on the opposite seat,
As it were by some horrible freak of Fate,
With the only man in the world I hate,
But him—oh, him ! with an infinite hate !

With a mutual glance that tells no lies,
With an uneasy hateful glare,
We look into each other's eyes,
Then turn away with an ominous stare
Out of the window or anywhere,
So that we see not one another.

But our eyes keep meeting still,
And show the hate we fain would smother;
For as in love, so too in hate,
There is a power to fascinate,
Stronger than the strongest will.
Every station where the train
Disembogues its living freight,
Each would live a life of pain,
A life of care and desolate;
Almost death, and count it gain,
Could we only leave the train,
And so escape our dreary fate.
But we are both too proud to move,
And so we still keep sitting there,
'Till gone is every passenger,
Leaving us a gloomy pair,
All alone with our great hate.

O God! we two alone together!
Is it not the strangest fate,
We two sitting close together,
Knowing that the merest feather
Might kindle all our deadly hate,
Now smouldering into fiercest fire?
And now and then we look askance
With a sudden vengeful glance,
Then carefully through the window-glass,
Seem to watch the country as we pass,

While on either side the banks run higher,
Till the road is narrowed like a funnel,
And the engine with one mad, long yell,
Completes the measure of our hell,
And plunges through a death-dark tunnel.

Now it is too much to bear ;
Darkness strikes the dreaded notes,
And with an impulse of despair
Our fingers clutch each other's throats ;
And silently with stifled breath
We reel and writhe in the gripe of death.

Hate ever is supernatural might :—
As we whirl around in maddening fight,
Our fingers twined in burning mesh,
Growing into each other's flesh,
The while I see, in the empty night,
By the aid as it were of some devil's light,
Colouring all with an ashen hue,
The fiery eyeballs glowing forth,
Mouths death-distorted with fiendish wrath,
And each one's face grown ghastly blue.
Dear God ! I see it but too, too well,
There in the dark, like a dream of hell.

Now comes the last, the fiercest rack :—
Death the Demon has unfurled
The horrors of the shadow world,
And then down an infinite vista of black,
Utterly drear and desolate,
We see ourselves in spectral strife,
Strangling in eternal hate,
For ever and ever one death in life.

Death has set his seal on fate !
One moment more, one moment more,
One last feeble gasp for breath,
And then our ghosts strive evermore,
In that spectral world of hate,
That endless pain, that endless death.

Ah God ! is this thine arm of might ?
Is it not then yet too late ?
Is this, indeed, thy glorious light
That comes between us and our hate,
Lifting us out of deepest night ?
The golden sun comes pouring in,
And struck with shame, we see our sin,
We loose our hold on each other's life,
Gaze at each other's blood-shot eyes,
And then fall back, too weak to rise ;
And it seems as if our long, long hate
Had spent its fury in that strife.

My heart has lost a nightmare weight,
And opens to a holier life,
As clouds, familiars of the night,
Crawl through the sky and quench its light.
Blacker and blacker, till at last
They burst in a mighty thunder-blast ;
Then in a whirl of wind and rain,
Roll back, and heaven is fair again.
Just so with this fell hate of mine,
Nursed in silence, gathering strength
Hour by hour, until at length
I grew a slave to its control,
Gave myself up, body and soul.
My own hate's property—in fine,
It my god, and I its shrine.

So now that tyrant hate is dead.
I lived in all the hate of life
Intensified, concentrated
In that one fearful whirl of strife.
We both arise and sit us down
As far away as we can be,
Eyeing each other sheepishly,
With half a smile and ha'f a frown,
While ghosts of days now past arise,
And heaps of ancient memories,
With yearnings for those earlier times

When each to each was more than brother,
Ere mutual wrongs and mutual crimes
Urged us on to hate each other.
'Twas after all no evil fate,
For love has ta'en the place of hate,
And I feel a fervent longing now
To call that very man my brother ;
And a mutual impulse moves us now,
For once again, I scarce know how,
Once again we clasp each other,
And thus with broken words and tears
Renew the vows of early years.

(*November* 1857.)

DIVINATIONS.

———•———

OH ! those sweet blue eyes of thine,
    With their trustful, wondering look,
  Tell me much, very much :
As they look up into mine,
I can read them like a book ;
And the passionate conscious touch
Of thy small hands locked in mine,
    Tells me much, very much ;
Trembling, thrilling through the calm,
Strong pulses of my rude rough palm.

Those dear little rose-red lips of thine
    Tell very much to me ;
As they move with a scarce perceptible stir,
    Which only I, who love you, see ;
A half tremor, a quiver supprest,
Only just motion enough to aver,
How the little heart flutters beneath the white breast,
The throbbing heart in the white, white breast.

In all you do I can divine
　　Much, very much,
In the lightest word or thought of thine,
In the most unregarded glance,
　　In the accidental touch,
When our hands meet just by chance,
This one truth I can divine—
Thy soul is wholly lost in mine,
And all thy being flows to me,
Like a restless river into a calm sea.

(*January* 2*nd*, 1858.)

L O V E.

———————

YOU have lost yourself in me,
But I have found myself in thee.
Until you gave yourself to me,
And made my heart your dwelling-place,
My life was but a stagnant sea,
This blessed world a desert space.
My heart lay buried in a tomb,
A sepulchre itself had reared,
Until you came into the gloom,
And Joy, and Hope, and Love appeared.

All, all to me was void and drear,
All good seemed dying on its bier,
And I had grown so desolate,
That Love was withering into Hate,
That Hope was trembling into Fear,
And Fear was darkening to Despair,
Until you came with your dear eyes,
Blue glimmering through your golden hair,
Until you came with your dear voice,
Came of your own free will and choice,
Gave me all yourself to prize,

And taught me, Love dwelt everywhere.
Daily as you grew more dear,
Self ceased to be the central line
Round which all thought and action turn ;
The life that I must live grew clear,
And the nobler being yearned
To all things holy and divine ;
Yearned for faith, and hope, and love,
For God below and God above.
To you then life and love are due,
For I have found them both in you,
And in your light my heart unfurled,
Till, loving you, I loved the world.

(*January 2nd*, 1858.)

SONG.

———◆———

THE little town sleeps at the foot of the hill,
   With its twinkling lamps mocking the sky,
     While the train whirls by,
     With defiant cry,
Sending a shudder of fear through the still
     Far depths of the sky.

Of those lamps that are mocking the stars above,
Oh ! I wonder which doth shine on her,
And my thoughts, can they stir gossamer,
And tell her in dreams, that I and my love
     Are close to her ?

(*January 2nd*, 1858.)

DESPISE NOT.

———•———

THE meanest weed upon this earth of ours
   That blows unrecked of in the sod,
Lives by the selfsame thought as brightest flower.
      The thought of God.
   God cares for even the meanest,
   For the foulest, the uncleanest,
      As well as for the fair;
   And there is nought too lowly
      For our care;
   The noblest, the most holy,
      Have a duty there,
   And hourly grow more holy,
      In the radiance of that care.

MAN.

I STOOD in silence with a silent sky
Ablaze with stars as with the thoughts of God,
That filled my yearning being with a sense
Unspeakable of Glory and of God.
A strong calm joy possessed my restless heart,
An unknown power shed itself around,
And thought on thought rose up from star to star,
As on a glorious ladder of pure light,
To the longed-for presence of my imaged God.
Truth, I had scarcely dreamt of until then,
Or wildly grasped at with a feeble hand,
Grew living, actual as the perfect stars ;
And things but dimly imaged to myself
In the faintest twilight of a doubtful mist,
Took life and shape, put on the mighty real,
And dwelt for ever shrined within my soul.
" Ah !" said I then, intoxicate with joy,
" Why care we for the baser things of earth?
When evermore the pathless heavens glow,
And myriad stars point mutely unto God,
Why care we for ourselves or for each other?

M

Our joys and sorrows are not worth a thought :
We live, we suffer, die, and pass to God,
And then the grand Eternal wraps us round."
    I ceased to speak, and shuddered as I felt
The utter stillness of the earth and sky.
The while a voice within me thus did speak,
Spake thus unto the folly of my soul :
" God see they on the earth, and not in heaven,
A man 'mong men—not Ruler of the skies.
Let things in heaven take care of things in heaven,
And give thy reverence unto things of earth.
Be simply man ; be still more what you are,
Attain the measure of the perfect man."

    So then I knew that all things are
        Aptly fitted each to each,
    Man to man and star to star,
        Answering only each to each ;
    And perfect man, body and soul,
        Heart and head, and thought and speech,
    Is the only true and worthy goal,
        The highest man may ever reach.
    And perfect man has perfect love
        For the lowest thing upon God's earth,
    Dearer than all the realm above,
        Man's lightest grief, most trivial mirth ;
    For there is nought too mean and lowly
        For our care.

The most noble, the most holy,
Have a duty there,
And grow more than doubly holy
In the radiance of that care.*

* *Variation :*

The most noble, the most holy,
Grow doubly, trebly holy,
If they do their duty there,
In the everlasting radiance of that care.

SEEMING.

WE seem—we might as well be dead :
        To seem is worse than not to be ;
God only values things that are,
And that which is—which really is—
No seeming can unmake or mar.

'Twere lower far to seem a god,
Than but to be the smallest man ;
Man ought to have one only aim,
To be the very best he can.

However small the good we do,
That little good can never die ;
No after sin can injure it,
'Twill bear its blessing by-and-by.

For if a man do one thing well,
But one, he conquers in the strife,
And God has gained another son,
And all are richer for his life.

THE ENGINE DRIVER.

ROUND with the break! shut off the steam !
    There is the signal post, with its red
Long danger arm stretched stiffly out,
(The signal man is asleep, no doubt).
Press the whistle ! oh, what a scream !
Shrill enough to stir the dead,
Or frighten a lover out of his dream.
The red arm falls—there is now no fear :
On with the steam ! the tunnel is clear.
Ah ! how deadly cold ! it checks my breath,
So utterly black, so utterly drear,
With a rumbling, grinding noise like the roar
Of waves that crunch on the sullen shore ;
And we plunge, as it were, through an ocean of death,
And hear the rumbling cry of the waves,
As they hurl us down to unquiet graves,
In the hideous depths of their dreary caves.
Now the times I have driven this engine before,
I never yet felt this darkness more,
Here in this tunnel than otherwhere.
On with more steam ! loosen the door !

And let the light of the fire gleam
Gaily forth on the snow-white steam,
That rushes forth in one long stream,
One long rolling river of light,
Cleaving a path through the tunnel night,
As Hope might cleave through a life of care.
As Truth might dawn in a nation's night,
As Love might lighten a heart's despair.

See, there in the blackness, ever so far,
Glimmers a light like a glow-worm's spark,
Still growing and growing till sphered like a star,
It floats full orbed in the fathomless dark.
There—you can shut the firebox door,
For like some grand new thought, the light
At first just glimmering on our sight,
Keeps growing more intensely bright,
Increasing ever more and more,
Till the little spark, scarce seen before,
O'erwhelms us in a heaven of light.

Oh ! the joy to breathe this full warm breath,
Like a draught of some celestial wine,
As the sun god glows in golden glory,
While all seems like an allegory,
Some strange vision of life and death,

As we whirl along our narrow line,
As it were our appointed groove of Fate,
While I, the driver, am like Free-will,
With power to move and regulate;
And you, the fireman, Circumstance,
The god so many bow to—Chance—
Heaping fuel upon life's fire.
Yet I, as I said before—Free-will—
Commanding, ruling all things still,
Fuel and steam as I desire.

As we rush along this groove of Fate,
Whirling down life's iron race,
Slow or sudden—soon or late,
We lose ourselves in death's embrace:
And then, when all grows desolate,
When shivering in death's cold caress,
We crumble into nothingness,
Even then God's light gleams from afar,
The glimmer of our new life's star,
A world of life in every ray:
Death and darkness shrink away,
And we stand once more in God's own day.

(*January* 1858.)

SORROW.

——◆——

SORROW ! Most human of God's messengers,
        And so most dear of all that wondrous host
That pass unseen from heart to heart for ever,
We love thee, and we pity thy sad lot.
For thou dost wash our sins out with thy tears,
And anguish softens at thy gentle touch.
Yet still thy wounds can never more be healed,
And thine the anguish of perpetual sin,
Sin not thine own, but strangely linked to thee
As the pale moon unto this glowing earth.
Sweet Sorrow ! Thou dost teach us things divine :
Oft our first glimpse of Heaven is through thy tears,
A golden morning in a silver mist.
Yet unto thee that heaven is closed for ever :
Thou leadest us unto the very gates,
And then Love comes, and leads us unto God.

THE WEDDING.

"I 'VE left the bridal party to themselves,
The only merry wedding I e'er knew.
The hoary church grew young again in wreaths,
Festoons and garlands, mingled leaves and flowers.
The sober birds that haunt the weird tower,
Leaving their sermons on mortality,
Shrieked epithalamiums at the happy pair.
Nay, the very graves forgot themselves in flowers,
Like bridal beds ; while troops of happy girls
In snow-white muslin fluttering in the air,
With nods and whispers innocently wise,
Looked like spring days, all smiles and tears and
flowers.
But tell me why were you not there ? "

" I there !
Death would have been a far more welcome guest.
The lady mother would purse her yellow lips,
Try to look scornful, and look simply hideous,
While the old father, fumbling with his thumbs,
Would turn with helpless glances to his spouse.

The bride perchance would give a little shriek,
Turn red and pale, then drop off in a swoon,
Leaving the bridegroom with a long blank face,
A helpless stone.   This were a meet revenge !
Small fools, I think, would find a glory in it:
But strong men scout the dagger and the bowl,
They watch in silence, never heeding vengeance :
Deeds are their own revenge."

        " Your words are strange !
The day was merrier than most weddings are ;
The bride as brides should be, except when blushing,
A little pale, yet never a single tear."

" No tear, you say ?   'Tis better so ; her fate
Is past all grief, her thought too deep for tears ;
For if she be a woman, as I hope,
Nay, if she have one trace of womanhood,
This were the darkest day of all her life."

" What, do you love her, then ? "

         " I did ; but now
I cannot love her, and I would not hate."

" Your eyes belie you, then : they burn with love,
Or hate, or both perchance, I cannot tell.
Your deadened hands speak passion unsubdued.

And so you loved her ! Well ! that's over now ;
The girl is married, think of her no more."

" You're very moral, a foolometer,
To mete the worldly.   Now be a man !
Give a man's judgment, accept my hand,
And keep your morals till you hear the tale :—
I was a lonely dreamer of all dreams ;
All outward things, so they were beautiful,
Took place and semblance in my world of dreams,
And in this world alone I really lived :
In the outer world I seemed, in this I was.
Nature to me was like a gentle mother ;
I loved her beauty with that mighty love,
That intense worship, I have now for God.
The stern wild mountains were as if unmoved,
The river laughing for pure joy of life,
The sun-loved hills, the sombre woods and plains,
Were dearer far than God or even my own kind.
As I loved them, they seemed to love me too,
To teach me all the hidden mysteries ;
And not a leaf but had its truth to show,
And not a stream but told me all its thoughts ;
Yet in this—nay, even in truth itself,
I saw the beauty only, not the love.
I liked fair women with a strange cold love ;
I wondered at the beauty in their eyes,
And joyed to hear the music of soft lips ;

But more I knew not; never cared to know—
I loved their beauty only, and not them.
  " But there came one at last across my path
More beautiful than aught else under God ;
The realisation of my wildest dreams,
Herself a dream, more fair, more false than all.
Oh ! how I loved that high young thought of God ;
For all the beauty of the glowing earth,
And all the radiance of the spell-bound stars,
And all the dreams of unknown loveliness,
And all the mysteries of unspoken things,
And all the love then sleeping in my heart—
All centered in one mighty wave of passion,
One love for her—not only for herself,
But for all others just for her sweet sake.
Her beauty did so shed itself about,
That common things grew rarer in her light."

　　　*　　　*　　　*　　　*　　　*　　　*

CLIMBING THE MOUNTAIN.

1.

IN those pleasant summer days,
Leaving all the beaten ways,
Did I wander musingly
Up the mountains that arise
With their feet in the sea,
And their heads in the skies.

2.

Long I clomb the mountain's side,
'Neath the forests tall and dim,
Where the storm at eventide
Came and sang a grand old hymn ;
While I joinèd evermore
In the mighty tempest's roar,
Loudly voicing a wild throng
Of fancies into song,
That in the tempest's roar,
I must hear for evermore.

3.

In the forest tall and dim,
Listening to that solemn hymn,
Where the gums above my head
Threw their shadows deep and grim,
In the night I made my bed
By a fire, whose scornful light
Roused the dusky phantom night,
    From her lair ;
  Flung forth a ruddy glare,
  Scintillating, corruscating,
  In the darkness everywhere.

4.

Now often, whilst I lay,
Half awake and half asleep,
As the fire died away
Into ashes cold and gray,
Oh ! such ghostly sounds were heard,
That for fear my flesh would creep,
And if but a leaflet stirred,
Seemed it like a whispered word,
From the wizard realms of sleep :
From the caverns of the dreamy mind
And wizard realms of sleep.

5.

All day long I roamed the forest,
  Now in sunshine, now in shade,
Now through brake and thicket tangled,
  Into broad majestic glade,
Where on brown grass, flower bespangled,
  Golden sunbeams idly played
With the swift coquetting shadows,
  Sunborn phantoms of the glade.

6.

Oh ! that forest was enchanted,
And I wandered spirit-haunted,
  Till a mist fell from my eyes,
  And the beauty that there lies
  And the wisdom that there lies
In the earth, and in its flowers,
In the sunshine, in the showers,
In the cloud forms of the skies,
  Did reveal themselves to me;
Not in givings ever present,
But in glimpses evanescent,
All unlooked-for, iridescent,
  Outward blushing, suddenly,
As the maiden to her lover
  Shows the riches of her heart,

For the most part still concealing,
　With a half unconscious art,
Only now and then revealing
By swift glimpses, the deep feeling
　That is burning in her heart.

7.

But, at last, I left the forest,
Rose above this haunted forest,
And stood upon the mountain's brow,
　Looking proudly down
On a vast expanse of trees,
Undulating in the breeze,
Till they mingled with the seas,
　In a line of blue and brown.

8.

Oh ! the joy, the bliss of living !
　How it thrilled through every vein,
How a wild extatic madness
　Seized my heart and stirred my brain,
As I stood just under heaven,
　Gazing on the mighty plain.

9.

Golden, 'mid a sunlit forest,
　Stood the grand Titanic forms,
　Of the conquerors of storms ;

Stood the gums, as if inspired,
Every branch and leaflet fired
    With the glory of the sun,
In golden robes attired,
    A grand priesthood of the sun.

10.

All below me, all above me,
    All within me felt the light,
And the foulest things grew beautiful,
    And the dullest things grew bright,
In the glowing golden glory
    Of this all-pervading light.

11.

For through the bluely waving seas,
And through the brownly waving trees,
Through the earth and sea and heaven,
    Shone the sunlight like a god ;
Till from the skies above me,
    To the rocks whereon I trod,
Not an atom but was conscious
    Of a grand eternal God.
And I felt it, standing voiceless,
    As the sun set in the sea,
Felt one God in earth and heaven,
    One God in them and me.

THE GAME OF CHESS.

———•———

WE were playing chess together,
    Where we often played for hours,
In a long and old verandah,
    That was covered in with flowers.
Claspt was every rustic pillar
    In the jasmin's white embraces,
While amid them peeped the roses,
    With their laughing, blushing faces ;
And they filled the air with fragrance,
    With an audible low sound,
As though they sang to spirits
    Unseen in the air around ;
For surely there is never a flower
    But is loved by some sweet soul,
That drinks the sunbeam dew-drops
    From its pearly tinted bowl ;
That lies dissolved in colour,
    Its delicate fair sense
Yielding wholly to the flowers
    And their gentle influence.
And we hear an audible music,

As they mingle and are blent,
As they sink away in beauty,
  Die in colour, die in scent.
But I little thought of flowers—
  Wasted was their choicest bloom,
Wasted jasmin, wasted roses,
  All their delicate perfume;
For she who played at chess with me
  Was beautiful as summer dreams,
And her voice was the low music
  Of rippling silver streams.
And her eyes were deep dark hazel,
  Though their darkness was not night,
For soft and beauteous soul-beams
  Turned their darkness into light;
And when they saw her ruby lips,
  The roses, merry wanton elves!
Were suffused with deeper blushes,
  Thinking that they saw themselves.

No wonder then I little cared
  For flowers ne'er so choice and rare,
When she, who played at chess with me,
  Was so supremely fair.
However, 'twas my turn to check
  The sovereign of the snow-white band,
When I left the game I know not how,
  And seized instead her whiter hand.

I held her thrilling hand in mine,
  Which, though 'twas ne'er so lightly prest,
Kindled all the love and passion'
  That had slumbered in my breast.
All that long day we spent together,
  In our pleasant low recess,
Talking softly to each other,
  But not about the chess ;
For though we talked and smiled and blushed,
  And mingled many a shy caress,
Like fickle mortals that we were,
  We quite forgot the chess.

THE OLD YEAR.

WAIL! all wail, for the death of the year,
    The gloomy, the sorrowful death of the year '
List awhile to the sobbing blast,
How it howls and moans as it sweepeth past;
And see how it scatters the leaflets sere,
Ghosts that haunt the dying year,
That haunt the bed of the dying year !

Mourn ! all mourn for the death of the year,
The gloomy, the sorrowful death of the year !
The purple earth, both by day and night,
Is ever dressed in her robe of white :
And the sky is covered with leaden clouds,
Wrapping the year in its sable shrouds,
The dying year in its sable shrouds.

Mourn ! all mourn for the death of the year,
The gloomy, the sorrowful death of the year !
The trees of the forest, all bleak and bare,
Shine and shake in the wintry air ;

And the withered leaves that are strewed around
Are a garment to cover the barren ground,
A mourning dress for the sorrowing ground.

Weep ! all weep for the death of the year,
The gloomy, the sorrowful death of the year !
The raindrops fall from the weeping skies,
And night draws a veil o'er her thousand eyes ;
Whilst over the earth the fog banks fall,
To make for the year a funeral pall,
For the year that is dead, a dreary pall.

THE "PARKI."

N EW beauties bloom at every turn,
    New life comes with the freshening breeze
That rustles through the curling fern,
And whispers to the happy burn,
    The far-off message of the seas.

The plain is like a lake of light,
    While lines of wood of darkling hue
Form here a cape, and there a bight,
Then slope away from height to height,
    To vanish in the distant blue.

O'er ferny slopes and rushlands low,
    Bird-like shadows swiftly pass;
As white-wing'd cloudlets come and go,
Or mingle in the sunlit glow,
    On terraces of waving grass.

There stretched but now a dreary waste,
    To-day, so richly fraught with life,

For snake-like forms were interlaced,
And grim smoke-spectres darkly chased,
  Or mingled in fantastic strife.

All bare and black, and black and bare,
  Nor sun nor moon to glad the sky ;
And heavy was the stagnant air,
Like one borne down with weight of care,
  Who only lacks the strength to die.

Oh ! here I think the preacher's art
  Might surely find a parable
Of life.   When early dreams depart,
Hope dies, and leaves the widowed heart,
  That might be almost dead as well.

Yet in the ashes of the past,
  Experience sows the seeds of truth ;
While reason tempers passion's blast,
And suffering melts in love at last,
  To usher in the second youth.

This second youth is youth indeed,
  When perfect love meets perfect trust,
And beauty lives in every weed,
And in the meanest human need,
  The spirit sanctifies the dust.

As knowledge grows, so manhood earns
  For pleasure yet a wider range;
To deep delight mere wonder turns,
The brain's creative impulse burns
  With thoughts the future would not change.

Then what though I be growing old?
  I still may keep the living truth;
And even in the common mould
May search, and find life's grains of gold,
  And win from them perpetual youth.

Lyell's Creek, Buller River, New Zealand.
  October 3rd, 1863.

IN A BOAT.

Suggested probably by floating down the Buller River in a
canoe.

———•———

L IKE the music of her feet
      Is the beat
Of the wavelets on my boat,
      As I float
Down the ever-widening stream,
With my dream, my life-long dream.

Myriad stars upon her brow
      Glitter now,
Intertwining bridal pearls
      With the curls ;
Golden curls that wave and float,
Wing-like round the foam-white throat.

So ! I hold thee thus at last,
      And the past
Is all forgotten in the beat,
      Wildly sweet,
Of this dear true heart of thine,
Answering throb for throb to mine.

And this heart, so deeply true,
    Bids adieu,
In the bliss of utter rest
    On my breast,
To the vanished sea of years,
Wild with passion, salt with tears.

There is one whose indrawn breath
    Mutters death ;
As the scorching touch of fate
    Baffled hate,
Baffled love is branding now
Hideous wrinkles on his brow.

Soul and body overwrought
    With one thought ;
Vengeance, born of black despair,
    Sitting there,
Brooding over some fell scheme
To destroy us, my heart's dream.

Thou, dear darling, let him scheme,
    For the stream
Bears us swiftly on our way
    Toward the day ;
Where, beyond the secret sea,
Life and love wait thee and me.

Lyell's Creek, N. Z., 1863.

SUMMER WINDS.

O H ! summer winds that shyly come,
    And twitter round the lichened eaves,
And flutter with a lazy hum,
    In and out the listless leaves ;

Like you, I loiter life away,
    Just flirting with this world of ours,
Amid its pains, its pleasures stray,
    Nor grasp its thorns, nor pluck its flowers.

Perchance I smile at human joy,
    Perchance I sigh at human woe ;
Yet seem they but a curious toy,
    A puzzle worth the pains to know.

For outward things but minister
    To feed a life too much apart ;
And passion scarcely seeks to stir
    The untried depths of mind and heart.

Yet, summer winds ! a time comes when
  Your strength will grow for good or ill;
To work the work of many men,
  And shape your forces to their will.

I too would live before I die ;
  I too would leave a something done ;
Ungyve a truth, uproot a lie—
  No matter what, so rest were won.

I yearn to feel the pulses play,
  The life that burns in every vein,
The strength that works in perfect sway
  Of thought and action, heart and brain.

Away, then, unsubstantial dreams !
  Henceforward I must live my life ;
The world has need of me, it seems :
  My part is vacant in its strife.

Whate'er my part be, great or small,
  I care not if I sink or soar ;
The meanest fly on yonder wall
  Has its own use—what can I more ?

Ararat, Victoria, 1865.

A DREAM.

I N the stillness of the midnight a vision came to me,
And I thought that I was sailing o'er a wild and
boundless sea ;
A storm was on its waters, and with fearful fiendish
din,
The billows strove which should be first to suck my
frail bark in.

Across the sky sped thunder-clouds, in masses grim
and black,
Save where a streak of livid fire revealed the lightning's
track ;
And to my heated fancy, the thunder's awful roll
Seemed like God's voice proclaiming vengeance on
my soul.

As when the moon shuts out the sun, deep darkness
fills the air,
So o'er my maddened spirit fell the blackness of
despair ;

But still I tried to steer my boat, as on the waves she
    tossed,
Until I saw 'twas all in vain—O God! I cried, I'm
    lost!

Scarcely had I spoken thus, when hushed was noise
    and riot,
The tempest's stormy rage was quelled, and all was
    still and quiet;
In wonderment I raised my eyes, and saw that it was
    thou,
Who, like a guardian angel, stood upon my vessel's
    prow.

   *   *   *   *   *

The scene was changed, and thou and I
Were wandering 'neath a moonlit sky,
Where stars, in many a brilliant cluster,
Shed their soft delicious lustre,
Till all the enchanting fairy scene
Glistened in their silver sheen.

But oh! this scene was nought to me,
For I could only think of thee;
And dearer far, Love, were thine eyes
Than all the splendour of the skies.
And sweeter far to me thy words
Than the softest song of birds.

For, oh ! in accents soft and low,
They told me what I longed to know ;
They told me that thou lovedst me
With love as deep as I loved thee ;
And sealed was this my rapturous bliss
With a mutual fervent kiss.

THE RIVALS.

JOY and Despair were brothers : Joy, beautiful
And glorious as the summer sun at morn,
Made all things brighter that he gazed upon.
Despair, who was in all things like to Joy,
Yet unlike as the mocker to the mocked,
Showed like the summer sun in dog-day glare,
And all things withered 'neath his evil eye.

Now both these brothers loved one maiden, Sorrow,
A gentle spirit, tremulously strong,
Pale as a star, with wondrous innocent eyes:
Before those eyes all evil shrank abashed.

Out of their love for this dear maiden Sorrow,
There grew a mighty hatred to each other.
The hate and love, commensurably strong,
Became yet more intense as time went on,
Until it flamed into a furious war.

Now Joy came girt in beauty and in strength :
A smile of hope looked calmly from his eyes,
A mighty scorn sat grandly on his lips ;

And his clear laughter rang so merrily,
That all things laughed for very sympathy.

Despair came to the battle girt in strength;
A smile that showed like hope, yet was not hope,
Sat glaring in the depths of his wild eyes;
Fierce scorn sat withering on his sneerful lips :
Like Joy he laughed, but with so grim a laughter,
The hills and valleys echoed it in groans.

Joy, filled with certain hope, struck blow on blow.
That flashed like sunbeams through the tossing air;
Despair fought wildly, blinded he with madness,
And every blow he struck he grew less strong,
Till, slowly shrinking to a hollow show,
He howling fled and sought the wilderness.
And evermore he dwells in desert places,
Uttering his curses to the careless stars;
Or wanders like a spectre through the world,
Searching out desolate souls and desert lives,
Or crouching in the depths of some sad heart,
Sits brooding o'er the memories of his shame.

Now Joy triumphant left the battle-field,
And took the maiden Sorrow for his bride,
And hand in hand they wander through this world,
Striving to win by their sweet influence
Each human heart to perfect peace and love.

Now Joy and Sorrow never work alone :
Joy never fills a heart with his own soul,
But Sorrow sanctifies it with a tear ;
And Sorrow never melts a soul to tears,
But Joy illumes their sadness with his smile.
For Joy and Sorrow are so wholly one,
Through the full union of their perfect lives,
That Joy is but the masculine of Sorrow,
And Sorrow but the feminine of Joy.

YEARNINGS.

A H ! would that I were with you, Sweet !
  Or would that you were with me here,
Lingering by this silver mere
That breaks in music at my feet :
Ah ! would we were together, Sweet !

The rushes bow to meet the lake,
I hear their hushed despairing strain ;
I hear the ripples answer make,
Low with passion, fierce with pain,
" We cannot meet—our love is vain."

This strain seems like hope's funeral knell,
For is it not so with us, too, Sweet ?
Might we not sing this song as well ?
" We live, we love, yet never meet,
Ah ! meet not, though we love so well."

It seems I have grown weak of late,
I spoke but as a love-sick fool—
I cannot be so mere a tool ;

It must be mine to conquer fate,
Yours, dear, that harder task—to wait.

'Tis not for me and thee to pine,
For surely, dear, a will like mine,
More surely yet a love like ours,
Must have a power almost divine,
To wrest from fate life's golden hours.

Then, dearest, let us act, not dream,
And love will make our labours sweet,
And all our common duties seem
But points where our two lives may meet,
Ere yet they flow in one full stream.

But still, God knows, 'tis hard to bear
This fruitless love, this baffled hope ;
And, all heart-weary with my care,
I sometimes lack the strength to cope
With the numbness of our old despair.

(1862.)

NATURE'S INFLUENCES.

1.

THROUGH deep and mighty forests
  I dearly love to wander,
See Nature as she dwelleth there,
  And on her marvels ponder.

2.

I love to watch the glorious sun,
  Uprising from the sea ;
Throughout my soul his beauty sends
  A thrill of mystery.

3.

I often look from the mountain top,
  Into the glowing west,
Where, 'mid clouds of gold and crimson,
  He seems to sink to rest.

4.

I love to see the blue gums stand
   Majestically tall ;
The giants of our southern woods,
   The loftiest of all ;

5.

When every leaf, and branch, and bough,
   Awakes to life and motion ;
When the whole forest heaves and sways,
   Like the waves of some vast ocean.

6.

'Tis then I feel throughout my soul,
   Its beauty so sublime ;
As when the vast eternity
   O'erwhelms all space and time.

7.

And these are all within my heart,
   Sources of pure delight,
Of high and holy pleasures, such
   As few men know aright.

DIRGE.

OVER the sea
Exultingly,
The cruel cold wind, with his icy breath,
Comes from the dreary regions of death.
Over the sea
Forebodingly;
While the waves roll up on the dull bare shore,
With a voice that calls from the sullen roar,
Death evermore!

This night last year
I wandered here,
Weeping and watching the long lone night,
Till the moon arose with a pallid light
From the dim grey wave,
Like a ghost from the grave;
While the sea rolled up on the ashen shore,
With a voice that spake in a sullen roar,
Death evermore!

Him whom I loved with an utter love,
Better, far better, than God above !
    Oh ! the cruel sea
    Killed him, not me,
When the waves rolled up the sepulchral shore,
With a voice that called from the sullen roar,
    Death evermore !

THE STORM-KING.

———◆———

THE king of the storms is abroad to-night,
And the guilty moon is livid with fright,
As she hurries along through the misty hosts,
That haunt her path like accusing ghosts.

Ah ! the king of the storms is abroad to-night,
Sweeping on in mysterious might,
Robed in a robe of blackest night,
Of darkness fringed with a line of light.

Aye ! the king of the storms, how grand is he,
As he comes along in his majesty,
And breathes with the breath of his wind on the sea,
While the waves arise and circle his feet,
Till he lashes them down with the hail and the sleet,
And they writhe and hiss with the shame of defeat.

So he leaves the impotent ocean to rave,
And bury the wrecks of its own wild wave
In the dim grey depths of its unseen grave.
Yet though the storm hath entered my soul,

I hold it under calm control,
While he rushes on to the unknown goal.

Ah ! could I do so with the storms that start
From the mighty depths of the human heart,
See them, yet hold them as things apart :
Could I be quite calm as amid the din,
In this whirl and riot of storms within,
'Mid blasts of passion, and rage, and sin :
Then, indeed, I should have the key
That would open all men's hearts to me.

DIRGE.

THE air is damp with the dripping dew,
　And the earth is damper still;
The wind comes moaning sobbingly,
　With a moaning all bleak and chill.
The moon is moving across the sky,
　On a floor of cold white cloud,
And the stars they look so gloomily
　From their dim and misty shroud;
And a dreadful feeling comes over me,
　As I gaze on that pallid sky,
And I shudder as if I were now enthralled
　By the spell of a serpent's eye.
But no one knoweth, and none can tell,
Where to-night is Claribel;
For all the night long she hath been away,
Though to-morrow will be her bridal day.
But wherever thou art, sweet Claribel,
May the Holy Saints defend thee well!

SONG.

I.

DEAREST maiden, I am thine,
 And oh ! I know that thou art mine ;
I know thy heart is all my own,
Its every thought for me alone.
And though I see thy sparkling eyes
 Shed sunny smiles on many,
Yet still the smiles thou givest me
 Are different to any.

2.

This earth of ours looks cold and gray
When the red sun goes away ;
But oh ! how young and bright it seems,
When lighted by his rosy beams.
And so, when thou art absent, Love,
 My heart feels dull and drear ;
But oh ! how full of joyousness,
 If only thou art near.

3.

Well I know thou lovest me,
As ardently as I love thee ;
For even now, Love, as I speak,
The red blood rushes to thy cheek ;
And, dearest Love, thy gentle eyes
    Tell me more than words can tell,
A truth as dear as life to me,
    Maiden, that thou lov'st me well.

4.

Yes, yes ! I am for ever thine,
And, dearest, thou art ever mine ;
Thy loving heart is all my own,
Its every throb for me alone.
And though I see thy sparkling eyes
    Shed merry smiles on many,
Yet, oh ! the smiles thou givest me
    Are different to any.

LOST IN THE STORM.

———◆———

A BOAT skims swiftly on the heaving waters of
  the bay,
Whilst the white waves clasp her wildly, imploring her
    to stay;
But she flies from their embraces, never heeding
    what they say,
But proudly with the laughing wind she dances on
    her way.

In the stern a man was sitting, of clear eye and open
    brow,
He swept the oar with nervous arm, and watched the
    wayward prow;
Gazed at the cloud-filled heavens, and checked the
    eager sail,
Till the little boat sprang quivering right against the
    rising gale.

Ha ! look at the Table Mountain, the tall guardian of
    the town,
Look at the hoary monarch, how he scowls with
    darkening frown;

How he looms from out the cloud-bank with a dim
and spectral form ;
The old tyrant must be angry, we shall have his
wildest storm.

Down from the cloud-girt mountain swept the mighty
maddened blast,
. Stamped the white sail with fury, bent the quivering,
straining mast ;
While the man sat calm and fearless, swept his oar as
well as ever,
Kept his head above the waters with incessant strong
endeavour.

But in vain the waves rise hungrier, madder, in their
savage glee,
For already one has struck the boat, and they sink
beneath the sea ;
And in the ghostly moonlight, when the tempest is no
more,
Will the waves with mournful music cast them on the
glittering shore.

CHESS POEMS.

I.

FROM youth to age, how dear the game of chess,
How kind a comforter in our distress :
How sweet a solace, weaning us from pain,
Giving fresh impulse to the wearied brain !
How pleasant an amusement after toil,
A quiet recreation, and a foil
To the wild mirth of more extatic pleasures,
To the glad music of swift dancing measures,
To the mad galop on the breezy plain,
To the swift sailing on the joyous main,
To summer plunges in refreshing fountains,
To all the full emotions born on mountains,
When, standing up between the earth and sky,
We shout for very joy of being so high.
Ah ! many a time have I had cause to bless
The quiet pleasures of the game of chess.

II.

WHEN quite a child, before I knew
Anything except the name
Of the royal ancient game,

When I deemed that all was true,
When the wizard tales of yore,
And all their legendary lore
Of countless marvels, were to me
Truer than reality :
When with profoundest interest,
I listened to wild stories
Of knights, enchanters, giants huge,
Till my heart leapt at their glories—
Oh ! then the game of chess to me
Was a magic mystery :
I thought the men were really men,
King and bishop, pawn and knight,
Bound by some magician's power
In a spell of wond'rous might.
And when I saw grave men who scorned
All trinkets, toys, and baubles,
Who never played at whipping tops,
And didn't care for marbles ;
Ah ! when I saw them playing chess
 For hour after hour,
I marvelled what the men could be,
 And whence their wondrous power ;
Till a yearning rose within me,
 To know more than its mere name,
For the secret of the chessmen,
 For the magic of the game.

III.

I HAD been ill; night after night
I wandered into wildest dreams;
Roused were the sleepers with affright,
At the fierce terror of my screams.

I better grew; was wont to lie
Where the sun smiled on me for hours;
Where breezes with melodious sigh
Came laden with the breath of flowers.

I had a nurse, a fair young girl
With deep blue eyes of love and truth,
Shaded by many a clustering curl,
Rich with the golden light of youth.

And often would she sit with me,
And while I held her fairy hands,
Would tell me tales of mystery,
And stories of far distant lands.

But sometimes I would tire of these,
Sick still for very weariness;
Till once, when nothing else would please,
She taught to me the game of chess.

And I, with boyish eagerness,
Would play all day and never stir,
Partly for love I bore to chess,
Partly for love I bore to her.

Then in the pauses of the game,
She used to kiss me if I won,
And if I lost, 'twas all the same,
I had the kisses every one.

She's gone, the heroine of my song ;
Those full blue eyes another owns,
And all her kisses now belong,
They tell me, to a Mr. Jones.

Ah, happy Jones ! those eyes are thine,
And I perhaps may see them never ;
But to Caissa the divine
I'll pledge my fealty for ever.

IV.

I SPENT two years exploring mine own land,
Roving amid its forests and its mountains,
Tracing bright rivers from their ocean grave
Up to the wilder birthplace of their fountains.

But in the mountain was our chief delight :
We loved the narrow glen, and wild ravine,
Admitting only just sufficient light
To give a gloomy grandeur to the scene.

Then afterwards to climb the rugged height
And bask in the full radiance of the light,
Quaffing deep draughts of mirth-inspiring air,
Till laughed the wild free echoes everywhere,
And hoary rocks rang back, with youthful zest,
A joyous answer to each joyous jest.

And oh ! how pleasant, when the sun had set,
To light our fire by some swift rivulet
That dashed along amid enamoured boughs,
Breathing the murmured sweetness of their vows.

Oh ! passing pleasant was it then to lie
On the fern leaves, in a luxurious ease,
With the blue heavens for our canopy,
Fringed with green curtains of the dusky trees !

How pleasant then to play the game of chess,
To lie at rest in calm and silent thought
On strategy deep-laid and subtly wrought,
To watch the figures in strange loneliness,
To mark the pawns which one by one advance
To weave a merry and fantastic dance,
Whilst the red fire is glimmering in the night,
And wraps the pageant in a mystic light.

CHARADES.

———•———

I.

CHANT ye, my *first*, in solemn tones,
　For the souls of the mighty dead,
Who 'midst the terrors of my *whole*
　To their Creator fled.

The Christian host had won the fight,
　And when the slain were reckoned,
Ten thousand dead were found within
　The ramparts of my *second*.

Then chant my *first* in solemn tones,
　For the spirits of the dead,
Who 'midst the terrors of my *whole*
　To their Creator fled.

II.—THE LAMENT.

How dull I am—how dull I am—
　My *first* are all about me,
Oh, why do they protest to me
　They could not live without me?

Why did they make me take the vow,
Which made of me what I am now?

I fly for refuge to my books,
　　To music, and to painting,
But yet the day is sure to end
　　In whining, pining, fainting.
Ah! would to heaven I had but reckoned
The ills of being my *first's* sad *second*.

III.

I ROSE one morning at break of day,
　　And gazed across the plain,
Where far in the hazy distance
　　There came a warlike train.

By the sword of good St. George, quoth I,
　　My *first* will be here anon,
And we shall have barely time enough
　　To gird our armour on.

The battle was over, and I alone
　　Escapèd from the fight,
And my *second* was my hiding place
　　For many a weary night.

IV.

My heart is lonely, for oh ! to-day
My *second* has borne my *first* away.

Years have passed—and both again
Have crossed together the trackless main.

But my heart is lonelier now than ever,
For trifles light as air can sever

The bonds and ties of many years,
Begun in joy, made strong in tears.

And now, alas ! my *whole* is broken,
By one harsh word in anger spoken.

V.

I WENT one night to number nine,
   In something Terrace Upper,
To spend an hour with Doctor Rook,
   And stay to tea and supper.
At tea, of course, the ladies talked
   Incessant pretty prattle,
Diversified by scraps of news,
   And charming gems of tattle.

But after tea, when hushed was all
    The chatter, noise, and rattle,
The Doctor and myself sat down
    To wage a silent battle :
To fight a stern and earnest fight,
    In silence seldom broken ;
For my *first*, my *first*, was the only word
    By either of us spoken.

Well, so we fought for full two hours,
    And though disdaining quarter,
We had a twenty minutes' truce,
    For bread and cheese and porter ;
For serious talk with Mrs. Rook,
    For whispers to her daughter,
For pretty smiles, by way of thanks
    For a bouquet I had brought her.

But, supper over, once again
    We bid adieu to prattle,
And sat us down in solemn state
    To wage our silent battle.
But I soon lost, for the Doctor gave
    A regular thumping trouncer ;
" Ah, ha ! " cried he, " my *whole* is yours ;
    I believe I have done you brown, sir ! "

TO MY DEAR MOTHER.

(Sent on New Year's Eve, 1875, from the author's cottage
home in Ferndene Garden.)

———•———

THE year is dead ; each hour, each minute,
  No doubt had some new thought within it ;
Some for nought, and some for shame,
Some for glory and a name.

But dearest far, imaginings
Are not to us as nearer things ;
Loved ones sad and loved ones dead,
Little things they thought or said.

You have lost a mother true,
Sweet sister I, dear daughter you ;
You gained a son I feel will be
Good son to you, leal friend to me.

I too, your erring only son,
A tender woman's heart have won,

Who is of us, of our own race,
Who must supply our dear one's place.

We live, we die—lie 'neath the sod ;
Meanwhile be happy.   *So* praise God.

UNFINISHED POEMS.

UNFINISHED POEMS.

NATURE WORSHIP.

I WILL away this glorious Sabbath morn,
   I will away into the joyous woods,
While yet the hills are purple with the light
Which, like a robe, the sun hath cast o'er them,
As he uprises from his couch of cloud
In naked majesty. Oh, I will forth
While yet the town lies sleeping in the light ;
Ere these sleek houses flout the midday sun
In their unblushing whiteness. What a life there is
In the deep wood to-day ! The lightest leaf
Thrills with intensity of life ; while I—
I feel in every vein and every limb
The joyous ecstacy of mere existence.
In every pulse my full life beats and throbs
Like a full passion ; while my heart dilates
With new emotions ; and my joyous soul
Soars with unwonted thoughts. Ah ! this is life,
   indeed !

I pity those poor sinners in the town,
Drowsily rising from a weary bed,
And crawling dismally through glare and dust ;
But I the while rejoice
In this pure air, that is itself a worship ;
A very soul of joy here in this glorious church,
Beneath this spacious everlasting dome,
That bounds my vision with its radiant blue.
Here in the coolness of these forest aisles,
Where giant trees make arches overhead,
Rich with the tracery of leaves and boughs,
Woven with innumerable forms,
Beautiful here upon this emerald floor,
All tesselated with the loveliest flowers,
Whose odours rise like holy incense up.
Now will I bow my soul before my God
In silent worship; while the full-voiced wind
Shall sing great anthems to the forest elves,
And streams that gurgle in amongst the stones
Shall make a mellowed soft accompaniment
To the glad voices of aspiring birds.
How beautiful is all I gaze upon !
From the blue heavens to these fragrant flowers
That sink beneath my feet.   It seems a sin
To trample on their beauty ; they look up
Like gentle eyes, with a deep meaning in them ;
And so they seem to speak, as eyes can speak,

With many truths inwoven in their beauty.
The silent stars are eloquent, they say,
Telling of glorious things; and flowers too
Are surely eloquent with softer voice
And lesser meaning.   The stars are angels' words,
But flowers are a language formed for man.
I pluck them in great handfuls, and drink in
Their fragrant breath, then fling them to the earth
To wither soon away, yet not to die.
For nothing perishes : we do but change
Our mode of life, death but the time of change,
The neutral point 'twixt this life and the next.
I needs must think, as they look up to me
In their dear loveliness, that spirits dwell
Each in its own fair flower, drinking in
The sunlit dew, and bathing in the waves
Of viewless odour, trembling with the joy
Of light and colour.   Oh, were my senses pure,
Were I but less a body and more soul,
I feel quite sure that I should see or feel
A number of sweet souls, and filmy forms,
Each with a likeness to its separate flower,
Yet different: like as the soul is like
Unto our face, like as a thought is like
The lips that utter it.   What would I not give
Now to perceive the beauty of these elves,
That ever haunt me with a glimmering,

Q

A vague, dim dream that whispers their existence !
For though I am oft conscious of the presence,
I still can never see them.   So I am vexed
With uncompleted power, like to a man
Whose soul is vexed with thoughts he cannot utter.

TWILIGHT.

THE day we love has departed,
Has left the earth with a sigh,
Though his soul still glows in the heavens,
His heart still throbs in the sky;
Still burns in the western heavens,
Like love in a tearful eye.

The misty forms of even,
The beings that love the sea,
Descend from their homes in heaven,
In spirit mystery;
With weird-like, silent footsteps,
They come from the realms above,
To lie at rest on the throbbing breast
Of the ocean whom they love.

The mountains that an hour ago
Were lit with a crimson blaze,
Are bathed in the indistinctness
Of a magic purple haze:

Q 2

Are seen through a lustrous dimness,
  Mellowed to one rich tone,
Like a maiden seen through the mist of love
  With a beauty beyond her own.

The giant trees of the forest,
  Dusky and grim and tall,
Stand like frowning monarchs,
  As in the old time Saul
Stood in the might of the evil
  That robed him as in a pall.

Every one of the giants,
  Crowned with a dusky crown,
In his own increasing shadow,
  Grimly gazes down ;
Though the wind, like the harper David,
  Would lure away their frown.

The flowers are drowsily nodding,
  Damp with the dews of sleep ;
And trembling for joy at the dreams
  Which into their being creep,
And fill them with love for the breezes
  For whom they ever keep
A hiding place in the twilight,
  A quiet bower of sleep.

So the winds, this calm dim even,
  Sleep in their silken cells,
Wrapt in the cups of flowers,
  And rocked in the tremulous bells
That sway to an audible music,
  The bubbling music of wells ;

To the babbling music of elves,
  That run through the dreaming flowers,
Down the side of the valleys
  Into the spirit bowers,
Where blossoms fall on the water
  In rainbow-coloured showers.

Oh, what is this river music,
  Its tones, are they grave or gay ?
'Tis a sound of delicious sorrow,
  Of joy with the name away ;
'Tis filled with the soul of the twilight,
  The mingling of night and day,

Oh, my soul is attuned through the music,
  I muse on the thoughts it brings,
And yield myself to the vision
  Of multitudinous things.

TO ————————————

MY sweet, sweet child! my life's sole dream,
　　Lovely in thy girlish grace,
　　Of lithesome form and baby face,
So child-like, thou would'st almost seem
Too child-like for the double life,
The perfect woman, perfect wife,
Were it not that I can see
　　All the woman in thine eyes,
And all a woman's love for me
　　Looking through those glorious eyes,
Wherein concentrated lie
　　The nameless charm, the holy hue,
　　The deepest deep, the bluest blue,
The radiance of our summer sky.

MOONLIGHT.

B EAUTIFUL looked the forest, as the white moon
from on high
Shed light upon the glitt'ring earth, and through the
cool grey sky ;
It had a ghost-like beauty, a strange beauty of the
night,
A loveliness that charmed the soul, and fixed the
wand'ring sight.

The peppermints rose like pillars, with funereal
branches hung,
Where the dirge for the dead is chanted and the
mourning hymn is sung,
And often from amidst a mass of thick and leafy wood,
Bare and white, some lifeless trunks, like gleaming
spectres stood.

The branches of the weeping gum were waving to and
fro,
And they rustled on the midnight air, with a rustling
soft and low,

That fell on the ear like music, and at that tranquil
   hour,
Their strange unearthly chiming had more than
   music's power.

Now like a harp it sounded, now like a pleasant
   rhyme,
As of one of the ballad singers, who sang in the olden
   time ;
Yet oft amidst this harmony the hooting owl was
   heard,
And oft the wild cat's howling, as he seized some
   sleeping bird.

Half hidden by thick underwood, a streamlet gushed
   along,
And it seemed that o'er its waters moved the spirit of
   sweet song ;
So musical the sounds it made, as it leapt from stone
   to stone,
Rippling o'er its pebbly bed, with an ever-changing
   tone.

There was an open spot, close by the margin of this
   stream,
Where, silvering the darkness, came full many a
   dancing gleam,

Which seemed, when thus they mingled with the
  gloomy shadow there,
Like rays of hope enlightening the blackness of
  despair.

Here, out-stretched upon the grassy turf, a weary
  hunter slept,
While, like cool fans above him, the slender branches
  swept ;
His knapsack was his pillow, the yielding sod his
  bed,
And, like a bright blue canopy, the sky hung overhead.

THE COMING OF THE NIGHT.

BEAUTIFUL, aye, beautiful ! the coming of the night,

As gently with her ebon hand she shuts the eyes of sight,

While like a long white curtain drops the ever-changing mist

O'er the summits of the mountains, which the parting sun had kissed,

Till the tints of gold and crimson sink by slow degrees away,

All merging in one lovely hue, a faint pale tinge of grey.

And now from out her myriad eyes Night lovingly looks down,

Now reigns in all her beauty above the distant town,

While like a meteor blazing, the full moon comes in sight,

And seems to bathe the sleeping earth in floods of silver light.

And as above the tranquil scene I'm calmly gazing now,

I feel the quivering moonbeams come playing on my
    brow ;
Like gentle kisses seem they, from some being not of
    earth,
Who was with me in my sorrow, was with me in my
    mirth.

THE VISION: A FRAGMENT.

———◆———

WHAT art thou, thou beautiful vision ?
    Thou surely dost more than seem !
Thou art some spirit from Heaven,
    And not a mere exquisite dream,
Born of the mystical twilight,
    Voiced by the bubbling stream.
Oh, I know thou art more than all these,
    I feel thy magical might,
For my heart leaps up at thy beauty,
    As a river into the light ;
It throbs in the joy of thy presence,
    As throbs a star in the night.

APPENDIX.

APPENDIX.

LOG OF THE SEAGULL.

August 7th, 1861.—I left home about 6 P.M. and went on board the *Seagull* with Mr. Nicholas, who returned on shore with a man who had no blankets, and to whom we advanced the same. I found that the captain had gone away to tea, and was not expected back for a couple of hours; so being one hand short, I went ashore again to see if I could pick up a likely looking man anywhere about the wharves. I succeeded in the person of a fat phleg- matic German lad, had a cup of tea at the corner tavern with Nicholas and the skipper of the *Enchantress* oyster cutter, who wanted us to wait till the morning, and run him as far as Maria Island. I said good-bye, took my Dutch- man on board, was done out of half-a-crown by a water- man, turned into a bunk where, short as I am, I could not straighten my legs, and while we dropped silently down the river, fell into a dream, wherein I was planted in a bed of guano, and grew up to such a height that my legs would not carry me, and fell with a great crash: and waking, found the *Seagull* bobbing about in a calm.

Thursday, August 8th.—Was up on deck just as the stars began to fade, and found that we were near Cape Raoul, every pillar and pinnacle of which stood in clear relief against the orange-grey sky. By the way, I wish somebody would nvent some such colour, though very few women could afford to wear it. I do not admire this Cape so much as some do ; it seems to me rather fantastic than grand, odd than beautiful: behind us were the faintly blue snow-topped mountains between the Huon and Port Davey, looking more like clouds than mountains. About sunrise two more of our party showed themselves on deck, and were soon leaning over the bulwarks employed in a manner especially ominous to me, as I was by this time growing very uneasy as to the fate which awaited me; a mouthful of tobacco juice I swallowed (my pipe being stopped up) settled the business. The sea grew all colours of the rainbow, and, like the others, I sacrificed to Neptune. I could not quite manage a breakfast, but made up for it at dinner, by which time I was as well as ever. The wind, though foul and gradually freshening, was light, and so we had not much difficulty in rounding the Pillar. There certainly is a wonderful beauty about these great peaks of Cape Pillar; they looked like those great stone idols from the Assyrian palaces one sees reproduced in the Crystal Palace. I composed a few verses anent them, being idle; I will not insert them here, but put them into an appendix. On the top of the Cape, I noticed for the first time a remarkable pillar of rock from which the place takes its name; this rock can be seen at a great distance, and has exactly the appearance of a lighthouse. Soon after passing the Pillar, the character of the coast changes entirely: instead of the sharp perpendicular lines of the basalt, one finds the soft horizontal lines of the sandstone formation which crops out for some miles, till near the headlands of Fortescue Bay, where the basalt again becomes the chief feature in the landscape. The basalt is perhaps the sterner and grander, although it does look, as a sailor on board the *Seagull* said, "like everlasting flour sacks piled upon each other;" but the sandstone has all sorts of dim caverns, dark *gulch*-ways and mysterious dens, which give a depth of light and shade, and a delicate imaginative beauty, wholly foreign to the basaltic formation.

Thursday (continued).—Towards evening, the wind be-

came what sailors call a good stiff breeze, but unfortunately dead in our teeth ; so the skipper, thinking prudence
the better part of valour, took refuge in Fortescue Bay.
At the entrance to the harbour are three singular islands,
separated from each other and the mainland by only a
few yards of water. One of these is the most extra-
ordinary pile of rock 1 ever saw : about the apparent size
of the tower of St. David's at its base, it rises per-
pendicularly from the sea (water all round it) to a height
of from one to two hundred feet. It reminded me of
pictures I have seen of a mountain called Peter Bott, I
think. We caught some fish for supper after we came to
an anchor, that would astonish Hobarton amateur fisher-
men, and after a little yarning and so-forth, turned in for a
quiet night's rest on smooth water.

Friday, 9th.—Found, on getting up, that the *Enchantress*
cutter had also during the night or early morning taken
refuge in Fortescue. The skipper reported the breeze as
being very fresh and dead ahead, so it was no use
thinking of getting out of harbour till next day. Two of
the sailors and myself landed with an empty keg at the
head of a little cove into which two creeks ran. The land
between them was of the richest description, overgrown
with splendid timber and shrubs, blackwood myrtle, musk
and native laurel being the most conspicuous trees. On
our return we met a fishing-boat which had come in from
the deep fisheries near the Hypolyte rocks. They showed
a "trumpeter" caught at a depth of 60 fathoms, about
30 lbs. weight, and said they had several larger ones in
their well. In the afternoon the skipper and myself
dined on board the *Enchantress*, and a capital feed of
red "gurnet" we had. Fishing, talking, idling, and
sleeping occupied our time till Saturday, August 10th,
when we in company with the *Enchantress* made a start,
but in our case a false one, as we could not make any
way against the wind (foul as foul could be) ; and so, after

R

kicking about in a nasty bumping sea for some time without making any way, we ran back again to Fortescue. Went ashore, and brought off a couple of loads of dry wood. About dusk, the *Swan* cutter came in for shelter, and later a fishing-boat came in with some enormous fish, and lay alongside of us, while the fisher-men cooked their supper by a fire made in a huge three-legged iron pot, and a strange Rembrandtish scene they made too : the fire-light flickering and flaming in the wind, and lighting up their swarthy sea-doggish faces, then passing across the water to the *Swan*, whose rigging showed like a gossamer network against the massive blackness of the hills. Before I pass to Sunday's log, I may as well mention a wonderful fish we caught, and which I had skinned, meaning to keep it for Moreton Allport. It was something like a red gurnet in shape, with sharp fins above and below, red on the back, but a sort of silver colour on the belly ; it had four little legs (apparently), and two feelers or smellers projecting from the mouth, and above all two beautiful wings coloured like the eyes in a peacock's tail.

Sunday, August 11*th.*—Rain during the night had made the wind fair ; so hauling our topmast down as a precaution against bad weather, we left Fortescue about two miles behind the *Swan*. We soon overhauled her, however, and making inquiries as we passed about the *Edward and Christopher*, left her some miles astern. The wind was fair, the day fine, and the coast beautiful, making as pleasant sailing for us as we could desire. As we passed the first headland of Maria Island, we took leave of Mount Wellington, and the wind freshening, bowled away at a great rate towards the Schontens. We soon found that our boat was not fitted for the open sea ; the boom being about three or four feet too long, kept dipping every now and then into the water and jerking us to pieces. The night was very enjoyable, however, the moon making a river of silver in the waves that grew broader and broader, and brighter, till it lost itself in a dim cloudland. The men amused themselves with singing and yarning till about eight or nine o'clock, and then turned in ; but I lay listening to the waves and looking at the moonlight on the water, and dreaming all sorts of dreams, and setting them to a sort of mermaid sealike music, till getting well drenched with spray, I thought it as well to turn in.

Monday, August 12*th.*—I was awoke some time during the night or morning by the skipper coming to call one of the sailors, as the main lift had given way ; it was blowing pretty hard at this time, and a high sea running, with occasional heavy rain. Finding I could not be of any use, I went to sleep again : such sleep as I could get at least, banging about as we were. I was up on deck about day-break, and the scene was wild enough. Only one of my men showed on deck, and from him I learned that they were all wet down below, as, besides the spray that kept jumping over our quarters, we took in a good deal of lee wash, which found its way below in spite of battened hatchways. Of course I was wet through directly, and as it was very cold, the sail, and the rattling breeze behind us, were more exciting than enjoyable. We were unable to get any breakfast, except biscuit, which didn't require much cooking. We found, when we began to see the land, that we had gone a long way out of our course, the land being 40 miles off; so we had to haul more on our wind (S.W.), which did not add to the pleasure of our sail, till we neared the land and found ourselves in smooth water. We met a large barque steering for Hobarton under reefed topsails, and without a stitch of sail on her mizen. About sunset we were abreast of the St. George's Rocks. We intended to have gone between them and the main land, as there is a good passage ; however, the wind being light (a sunset lull), barely enough to keep us clear of the great tide rollers, we thought it the wiser course to keep well to seaward. The sunset was one of the most beautiful I ever saw, crimson and rose colour prevailing. It had a peculiarity which I may mention, namely, a great arch of rain-clouds like a crimson fringe spanning the whole. Crimson showers would be a novelty in a picture.

About 9·30 P.M. we made Swan Island light, and stood off well to the westward, not liking to enter Banks' Straits, one labyrinth of rocks and shoals, till daybreak.

Shortly after I dropped asleep on Monday night, I became aware of an uneasy motion which made it a tooth-and-nail business to keep in my bunk : and before long I heard the skipper come down and say, " Get up : it's coming on to blow fearful—there's a heavy sea now, and the wind won't be long after it." Now in the open I should not have cared much how it blew, as she would have laid to like a duck ; but here in this coil of rocks and reefs, with strong tides running we knew not how, and with no boat (barring a little dingy and a pair of paddles) to help us in case of grounding or touching a reef, a gale at night became a different matter. So I stepped up on deck to see how things looked, and was agreeably disappointed : there was only a jumping, boiling sort of sea such as would be the natural result of the ground swell from the morning gales meeting the strong set of the tides here over a foul bottom. So I went to bed and sound sleep again, till daylight began to break along the horizon, and then found myself close to Goose Island lighthouse. By-and-by, when the daylight grew broader and the island became visible, one by one we made out the beautiful peak of " Mount Chappell " rising above the long low shores of Badger, with the granite peaks of Flinders in the back-ground, blue against a many-coloured dawn.

We now changed our tack, but on attempting to gib found the mainsheet worn through to the last strand. It was most fortunate we found it out when we did, as had the last strand gone it would have been very awkward to have had our over-grown boom banging to and fro in a cross joggling sea. We were not long in splicing it (the mainsheet) and by about 8 o'clock a.m. we dropped our anchor under the lee of Mount Chappell. The skipper, sailor, and myself landed, though not without difficulty. I found that Mr. Thomas was away at Green Island, so I left the things I had brought him, as well as my credentials, with Mr. Geddes, his substitute here.

I saw Mr. Westbrook (a cousin of Mr. Westbrook in Hobart Town, Mr. Patterson's agent), and he promises me the use of his boat to land my things. I was then shown over the island or part of it. I had certain claims pointed out to me as good, and certain spots recommended for camping. There are only two boat harbours here, at least on this side the island, and of course it was important to camp near one of these, on account of landing stores, &c. I chose a spot under shadow of a great granite rock near Shag Boat Harbour. This said harbour is a most singular place, like a dock inside; the entrance is tortuous and intricate in the extreme, there being only a narrow passage (a few feet wide) between a perfect tangle of rocks, sunken or otherwise; one might fancy that an old sea-king had built it as a maze for some bewitching mermaiden, Rosamunda; pretty and pleasant it is, with glittering rocks and richly painted lichens, a white sea-sand, and kelp weed monotonously rising and flashing and swinging with the ebb and flood of tide; but outside, rocks and breakers, reefs, and gulch-ways enough to baffle any jealous sea Eleanor.

Went back to the *Seagull*, had a snack, brought four men on shore to pull the boat, and on crossing to Shag Harbour, was surprised to see the *Edward and Christopher* arrived, being brought into the dock by long sweeps and a tow boat. Mr. Smith was on board, and I was glad to see him, as, besides having a companion in him, I should have been afraid to take up my claim without his advice.

I received letters from my mother and Nicholas, also stores of various sorts and newspapers.

We started at last for the *Seagull*. I did not pull myself, there being a man to spare in the boat, but sat on the gunwale, reading my letters, when all of a sudden the boat caught in the break of a surf wave on a sunken rock, and rose straight on end. Fortunately, however, we got clear before the next wave came, with no worse mishap than a boat half-full of water and a good wetting. We put two water-casks with the things into the boat. I did not start with them this trip, as I had a few things to pack up and intended going on shore in the dingy. It seems that the tide was so strong that they could not get anywhere near the harbour, and so went into a sort of passage or gulch way in the rocks—an awkward place to get into sometimes, but at this time safe enough. I started away in the dingy to prevent them landing the things there, but was too late ; the water-casks, however, could not have been landed there under any circumstances. I obtained leave from Mr. Westbrook to take his boat back to the *Seagull* to be in readiness for landing the first thing in the morning. So leaving a man, an old soldier who had been used to sentry work, to take care of the things and himself also, as best he might with the help of a sail and a little firewood, we returned to the cutter about sun-down, intending to stop on board all night. The wind had a word to say in the matter, however, for it came on to blow hard from the north-east, and the sky soon grew black with serious-looking clouds. Now with a north-east gale our anchorage was unsafe, being open to the wind in that quarter ; so there was nothing for the *Seagull* to do but to cut and run either for Lock Rist Bay, or Flinders, or Green Island anchorage. The boat we had from Mr. Westbrook was now in our way rather, as we could not tow it after us very safely; so without taking our tea, though it was all ready, we threw blankets and what necessaries we could into the boat, and left the cutter.

It was fast getting dark; however, I knew my way into a little boat harbour just above the gulch way, where they landed the things pretty well, and thither we arrived in the dark safely enough. Now came our difficulties in real earnest, as there were only five of us to beach and unload the boat in the dark, and with a tolerable surf running. I had lent the skipper one of my hands to help him on board the craft; and another was with the things not above a hundred yards off, but still out of reach in the dark, as the place was one heap of rocks, holes, ferns, nettles, and ba-sullas. After many failures, we succeeded in rolling the casks out of the boat though not without fingers jamming and breaking the lining of the boat. By waiting for the high surf wave we managed to drag the boat some little distance up the shore, till at last, pull as we would, she only buried herself deeper into the sand. We then tried a "dodge" known as "cutting her in-set up:" that is to say, lifting her round, first by the stem and then by the stern, and then the bows, and gaining a few inches each cut for some time, till we got her into loose sand and were fixed again. We put her head straight, and as we intended to sleep on the sand, and have one watching always, we thought her pretty safe. Now the next business was to light a fire, dry ourselves, and have tea. Neither of these appeared very easy. We had only a few matches, some half dozen amongst us, and the wind was very rough. However, we made a hole in the sand, and cut up a piece of deal we found into splinters, all hands foraging about for such dry rubbish as there was—when one of them was accosted with a " Who are you?" and " What do you want?" and Mr. Phillips came up and asked why I didn't come up and tell him my difficulties ; had all his men down to help us haul up our boat, and housed us all just as the first burst of rain swept across the island.

The first thing next morning (Wednesday) I went to look after my old soldier and the baggage. He had managed to keep himself and the flour pretty dry during the night, and though he had had nothing to eat since dinner the day before, was well compensated by a drop of comfort I brought him.

The day was very fair and the wind light, but still the *Seagull* did not show out any where. So I cut a road from the little cove where the things were landed into Phillips' track, and lumped the baggage as best we could to our camping place. I was on board the *Edward and Christopher* somewhere about noon, when Mr. Geddes and Mr. Phillips came down to see me. They told me there was a large fire on Flinders (I had seen it an hour or two before), and that no one was living anywhere near there, and it was always considered a signal of distress in these parts. They feared some mishap had happened to the cutter during the night, as it had been dark and stormy ; and a man not used to the tides, which are very strong and " contrairy," might easily come to grief. The end was, that wolfing a hasty dinner, we started (Mr. Phillips, myself, and three or four men) in a whaleboat for Flinders. about seven miles off.

When about half-way the smoke took a sudden start, as if we were seen by the fire-makers, and as if they had piled up fresh fuel to make sure of attracting our attention. Our progress was but slow, as the wind, which came in little puffs and calms, was too much ahead to permit us to fetch the land without tacking. At last we made the land, but some distance from where we had seen the smoke, which seemed to have ceased altogether before we reached the shore. We dropped kedge anchor down as a precaution against surf waves, and making a long spring, another man and myself landed all fours on the granite. We went some distance without finding traces of fire, but at length, when I was about to give up the search, I noticed a faint smell of burning, and literally following my nose, we came to a plot of burnt and still smouldering scrub. We were unable, on a short survey, to find any traces that would lead us to a conclusion as to by whom and for what purpose the fire had been lit : it was too early in the year for spontaneous or accidental fires ; neither was it the hunting season : so we went back as wise as ever. We went to the rock we landed at, when the boat came to us, but without dropping her kedge first. As we were about to make a jump on to the rock and thence into the boat, a great sea came boiling over, which made us think twice about it; so the boat went to another spot, and I landed knees first on the bows, my companion geting into the boat I don't know how, though he had to get out again pretty quickly, and stick his feet against the rock ; for there we were hard and fast, with great waves roaring up behind and over us. I did not see much of what went on, as I was in the bows, pushing with all my might. I heard Phillips' voice, crying, " Pull, my lads—lift her, boys ! Hang you, pull, man ! another wave will sink her." Well, we got off at last, and turning round, I saw that we were nearly filled with water. " Overboard with the ballast and bale away, men, with boots, pannikins, anything you have ! " was Phillips' order, and before long we were sailing before a fine breeze, thankful that matters were no worse ; for besides losing the boat and probably drowning a man or two, it would have been absurd enough, after having gone to assist supposed shipwrecked men, to have been ship-wrecked ourselves. We returned to Mount Chappell, about dusk, puzzled both as to the fire and the *Seagull*, but with a mighty keen appetite for food and fire.

It is a curious fact, that about every ninth or tenth wave

three great waves came up far larger than the average.
We happened just to catch one of these giants, and a
narrow escape we had of it ; a few seconds would have
engulfed us. Talking about the ninth or tenth wave,
Maturin, I think, in one of his tragedies (Bertram ?) talks
of the " tenth wave " of woe or despair, or some such,
meaning the last pound that breaks the donkey's back,
agony—piled up, in fact. That morning (Friday) there
was nothing to be seen of the *Seagull*, so Phillips
and I and a telescope went up to the mountain to
see if we could make her out anywhere. The view from the
summit was magnificent, but nothing could we see of the
cutter, till at last when we became used to the glint of the
sun, we saw her coming up Fork and Kid Bay right in
the sunlight, which had at first prevented our seeing her.
We were delighted, as may be imagined, for we had
almost given her up for lost. She came into the anchorage about 10 o'clock, and we lost no time in sending a
boat to unload her. I did not go myself this trip, being
busy prospecting, and on going over about 12 o' clock
I was astonished to see what little progress the boat
had made, and wondered why they kept so far from shore.
Sometime after this I was smoking with Mr. Geddes in
" Paling Palace " as we call Phillips' hut, the only wooden
tenement on the island, when I heard cooeing, and found
the men not only no nearer the harbour, but a great deal
farther out in the current. We soon saw what was the
matter ; they were heavily laden and besides were towing
three water casks, against which the tide setting proved
too much for them. As before, I had recourse to Phillips,
and we went off in his boat to help them. They seemed
dead beat when we came to them ; had been pulling, they
said, two hours without gaining an inch. However, there
being a good breeze to sail with and oars besides in each
boat, we soon succeeded in getting boat, casks, and all
into the little harbour opposite Phillips's, about a mile from

Shag Boat Harbour, our ultimate destination. With regard to the *Seagull* and bush-fire mystery, it appears that the skipper having sails to repair and tackle to look after, and finding some remnants of a wreck besides, thought it better to lie quietly at Fork and Kid: the fire had been lighted foolishly enough by a sailor named Steere, though the skipper had told him it might cause him annoyance. Poor Steere, a great humourist in his way, was abused right and left by friend and foe, till he and the *Seagull* set sail for Hobart Town about an hour before sunset.

On going down to the beach on Friday morning, I found the casks adrift; however, by wading waist deep in water, we secured them again, and towed them to their resting place. I went with the men the first trip, and by keeping as close to the shore as possible, avoided the tide rip and arrived safely, without any other mishap than getting foul of a sunken rock or so. Friday night we all took up quarters under our canvas, having had shelter at Phillips' hitherto. Our party consists of eight men altogether. I being Monarch and Mr. —— (Smith we call him) Prime minister. About myself, the less said the better; but Mr.—— may well occupy a few words. A scientific man, somewhere about seventy, I suppose; in his early days connected with the American embassies both during the French war and the late American war : a Frenchman by birth, but long resident in the United States, Holland, London, and these colonies, he seems more cosmopolitan in his notions than his countrymen generally. He is a very agreeable man, witty, and abounding in anecdote, and with reminiscences of the past which would make a pleasant volume of historical gossip. He is our wise man, and goes by the name of Doctor. The cook of our party is a somewhat remarkable character, one of the class of men commonly denominated geniuses—a very useful class to pick bush cooks from, as they generally know a little of everything and are handy about a place. This cook of ours is a cabinet-maker by trade, has been in the army, and is now in the city guard, absent on leave. He has a wife, a garden, and a batch of of children, I believe, in Hobart Town. He cannot pronounce his R's and L's, but makes W's of them all ; so how he manages to drill his men I cannot tell. He must say, " Wight weg forward." He often makes ridiculous mistakes, owing to this absurd peculiarity. The other night we were talking about Baron Park. The cook declared he (Park) was Chief Justice of Ireland in 1852, and on our disputing it, he said " Oh ! I'm sure of it, " we got his wife at home," meaning his life, of course. Then I have another old soldier, who, old soldier-like, is a desperate grumbler. I made him cook for a day or too, but soon sacked him, and sent him to the pick and shovel, where he works well enough. He says he is only forty years old, but is always remembering things that happened fifty years back ; he has but two teeth or tusks, like a pair of sentries, at either side of an ample mouth. On board the *Seagull* it was amusing enough to see him try to make a meal of biscuit, growling and swearing all the time. Of course his teeth and himself were butts for the party. They used to tell him he kept one for show and another for use, and many similar pleasantries. The chief fool to the party, however, is a German called " Dutchy," who was chosen for the office by the party the first evening we embarked. He is fair, phlegmatic, with an idiotic laugh, and an expression of face that sets one grinning directly ; he can sing a song, and has an indiarubber back. He can pick up a stone from the ground with his teeth without bending his knees. He is constitutionally lazy, what the men call " a fire spaniel." Jokes practical and otherwise are reserved chiefly for him and a man in Patterson's party—both these butts say good things occasionally. Like Sir John Falstaff, they are not only witty themselves, but the cause of wit in others. For the remaining three men, one is a fine, well-built German lad, used to whaling; the other two are natives—one an intelligent, stiff-built man, the other rather pale and weakly looking, but he had a fight with the strong German lad " Peter," and thrashed him, to my great surprise.

Saturday was a very bustling day with us all: what with the arrival of the Government schooner *Ira*, and the departure of the *Edward and Christopher*, and, what I was forgetting, the arrival of a whaleboat from Launceston, with Captain Shingle Short (I must suppress his real name, as my remarks may not always be complimentary), Phil Thomas (a half-caste man) and famous boatman, another man ycleped Bill. Captain (or rather Mr.) Shingle Short introduced himself to me and began talking at a railway pace about himself and guano, plentifully sprinkling his monologue with pieces of advice. He is a good-looking man, a little taller than myself—I suppose about five feet eight inches—with an off-hand, but not unpleasant manner.

The confusion owing to the departure of the *Edward and Christopher* was amusing enough : such rushing to and fro with notes, parcels, and messages, such inveigling of pens, ink, and paper ; frantic letter-writing everywhere. A varied assortment of writing desks—buckets and bowls, beef-casks and potato-bags. Captain Swan makes two desperate attempts to write to his wife in peace and under shelter, but fails—stands at last on one leg. goose-fashion, with a pencil and scrap of paper on the other. Can't get on fast enough. People shouting for him everywhere. A friend who has the pen of a ready writer, and can stand on one leg *ad infinitum*, comes to the rescue, and shares the conjugal secrets of Captain and Mrs. Swan. The skipper of the barque meanwhile, the wind being fair, longs to be off ; so shouts, implores, telegraphs, prays, swears, paces up and down, wild-beast like, loosens the sail, makes believe to go—but all to no purpose. Captain Shingle Short is not ready yet, he has important despatches. Time and tide must wait for our Mount Chappell despatch ; still another chance for dilatory husbands, sons, and friends: more letter-writing, more shouting, confusion worse confounded. Skipper Donald almost ready for the happy despatch. When Shingle Short boats off his dispatches, the barque is off and out of sight in no time. I went on board the *Ira* in the afternoon with Mr. Thomas, the surveyor, who regaled us with bread and cheese and rum. I promised to visit him with Shingle Short next day (Sunday) at Green Island. He (Mr. Thomas) gave me a Cape Barren goose which I took home, and which was eaten next day (stewed) with infinite relish. I will try and get some for you, but ours is a bad island for them. Their great haunt is about twelve miles off. They are near the size of a domestic goose, but have, I think, a finer flavour. We made a start in Shingle Short's whaleboat for Green Island, but came back again, as the wind was foul and the boat was not safe to beat with ; seeing it had a plank out, and it was too hard work to pull her against wind and tide. We borrowed another boat, but were too late in starting, and had to come back unsuccessful after all. Shingle Short entertained me with his lies and feats of prowess. I believe he never says a word of truth except by accident, and never deceives anyone but himself. He comes up to Sancho Panza's idea of a liar, if we may judge what that was by his description of a man of truth, viz., "one who never tells lies except it is to his advantage or he has a mind to." In addition to his mendacious qualities, he is the most egregious ass I ever knew : not without brains of some sort, indeed, but with cleverness enough to show the wonderful depth of his donkeyism, just as a rushlight would help to show you the utter darkness of a tunnel. When I attempt to comprehend this ass without end, I am lost, staggered, as though I were contemplating the distance of the most remote fixed stars. We came home cold and hungry, about sunset, and Shingle Short taking advantage of my eating with him, must needs make me read two quasi love-letters he had received, which any baby, moderately precocious, might have seen were a hoax ; and I had to listen to the history of his wife and the inventory of her numerous perfections. It would be a mercy if bores such as Shingle Short were strangled in the cradle, or deprived of the power of speech. Lynch law wedded to Phrenology might be of some service. I am pretty nearly the only person on the island who has not quarrelled with Shingle Short. I humour him as I would a madman, and seldom contradict a word he says.

On Monday we set fairly to work and nothing very particular happened for some days ; so I may as well give a description of the island.

If you take a map of Tasmania and look a little to the west of north, commencing at the N.E. corner of the island, you will see a small group called Chappell Islands, the Goose where the lighthouse is, Badger, and Mount Chappell. Mount Chappell is separated from Badger by a narrow passage about a mile in width. The Goose is about two miles from Badger. Of these islands Badger is the largest, and the Goose next in size, but neither of them attain to any considerable elevation. Mount Chappell contains 650 acres or thereabouts, is of granite formation, and culminates in two rocky pyramids, the loftiest of which is about 600 feet. There is no harbour for ships, and the anchorages are very insecure. The shore is very wild. Great granite rocks rounded and polished, piled one on the other in bold fantastic masses ; here and there are little strips of sandy beach. There are no trees on the island, but it is covered with a luxuriant vegetation, consisting for the most part of barilla, kangaroo apple, geranium, nettles, wild celery, chick-weed, and a kind of stunted acacia, pig's face (*Mezembri-anthemum*), a plant, a sort of *Corea*, known here as box, and in the more sandy portions everlastings, sarsaparilla, and tussac grass. Most of the plants here mentioned are useful in some way or other. An acre of barilla, a scrubby bush with lavender-coloured leafings, will produce a ton of potash, worth, I believe, about 14*l.* per ton. One hundredweight of barilla will saponify its own weight of fat. The pig's face is a good anti-scorbutic, it removes the irritation caused by nettles, for which we have frequent occasion to use it here ; it has a very tolerable fruit. Nettle-tops are nearly as good as spinach, the same may be said of mallows. The celery is very like the garden celery, both in taste and appearance, with a taste like carrots and a dash of lemon peel ; wild parsley too grows in abundance ; the sarsaparilla has valuable medicinal properties, according to Dr. Townhend ; the kangaroo apple, besides being a beautiful plant, bears an edible fruit, and geraniums have a most delicious perfume that scents the whole island ; the stems are thick, but seldom exceed a height of from one to three feet. The scenery of, or rather from this island, is very beautiful, and in many respects it is a very desirable place, but has, how-ever, one great drawback, a skeleton in the cupboard of super-extra ghastliness : Mount Chappell has fleas—I am wrong : the fleas have Mount Chappell. Legions of these savages attack us both by day and night. They must be cannibals who have suffered metempsychosis. Oh ! for a missionary to convert these black sinners, these devourers of human flesh, these guzzlers of human blood ! What do you think of one man catching a hundred in his flannel shirt, after a residence of two or three nights in the thatched huts the Straits people have for the birding season (our autumn) ! I caught about three dozen myself

in my blankets one day, and yesterday the cook told me
he caught fort᾽. I have heard a great deal about snakes
here, but have seen none. True, I don't go into the
scrub much, as besides being full of mutton-birds' holes
that one sinks into at every step, the nettles are desperate.
I.'counted twenty-five great white spots on my hands after
being stung by one of them; the irritation will last a
couple of days, unless cured by rubbing pig's face or some
such remedy into the stings. As old Bill (one of our butts
here), says, " nettles to home be savage, but beant half so
savage as theym be." There are innumerable birds all
about these islands. The "mutton" birds are expected
here about the 15th of September (this month), and it is
said that they come in such clouds as to darken the air.
I feel anxious to witness their arrival. The ground here
for the depth of six feet is one mass of bones, indeed it is
the decomposition of bones which forms the most valuable
constituent of the guano. From the associations connected
in one's mind with guano and mutton-birds, I daresay
you think there must be a perpetual stink here (sure, a
coarse word, but I know no other suitable). On the
contrary, there is a most delicious fragrance on the
island, owing partly to geraniums, I think, and partly to
some other herb which I have been unable to trace
hitherto. There are no animals on the island, except a
wild dog or two, wild cats, and a few rabbits. The insect
life is plentiful enough. I wish I had brought some pins
with me to preserve specimens, as I see many kinds which
are new to me.

About this time, to beguile the long evenings, wet days,
and so on, it was proposed to have a sort of journal.
Accordingly, Phillips, the officer, and myself issued a
notice, of which, as nearly as I can recollect, the following
is the substance:

S

THE GUANO GRUMBLER AND MOUNT CHAPPELL GAZETTE.

A company has been formed for the establishment of the above Newspaper, which will be issued in a weekly form, the first number appearing at an early date.

CAPITAL.

Pens, Ink, Foolscap, Brains, and Blotting Paper.

LIABILITY—Limited.

ASSURANCE—Unlimited.

TERMS (payable in advance) :—
  For Journal—One yard of Broad Grins.
  For Advertisements—Nothing per inch.

To CONTRIBUTORS.—All advertisements, correspondence, &c. &c., intended for insertion in the G. G. and M. C. G. must be deposited in the editor's Gunny Bag, which will be placed in a conspicuous position in or near the settlement adjacent Shag Boat Harbour.

VIVAT REGINA.

I must plead guilty to the parentage of this folly, with the exception of the idea about the gunny bag, which contains a local allusion you will not understand. Of course the language was polished up a little, as I merely write from memory. The scheme fell to the ground, owing to our population decreasing suddenly by about one-half. I wrote a rhyming prologue for it, which I will cut out of my pocket-book.

Some day during this week —Thursday, I think—Perry's boat left for Launceston, taking a number of Dr. Cronthus' men. I sent letters by her. On Saturday a topsail schooner, called the *Boindie*, arrived to take a cargo of guano for Paterson. The skipper brought me a letter and newspapers from Nicholas. On Sunday the skipper, whom I will call " Bluff," Shingle Short, the others and

myself, made another attempt for Green Island, and this
time with success. There we found the government
schooner just getting ready under weigh for Mount
Chappell, so as we had some thought of going to Kangaroo
Isle, we exchanged our boat for their whaleboat, which was
easier to pull, and there was no wind to sail with. Green
Island is a low island overgrown with nettles, which flourish
there in extraordinary luxuriance ; all the other plants on
the island would scarcely cover an acre of ground. It is a
complete rabbit-warren : you can knock them down with
sticks and stones as fast as you please. We brought away
a great many with us, which made a pleasant change from
our salt junk. We intended to have gone to Kangaroo to
get some geese, but had not time. However, before
starting, we saw some geese on a spot where there was a
possibility of surprising them ; so Shingle Short, who is
nearly as good with a gun as he is with the long bow—
which is saying a good deal—went after them, we remaining quiet, only motioning with our hands to him how to
proceed. He soon brought us back a fine fat goose ; he
told us he had wounded another, so we agreed to pull the
boat round while he walked across after geese. We had
not pulled far when we saw him motioning to us, and
Bluff, who was steering, descried a goose in the water. We
laid on to our oars as hard as we could, and soon came
up to him. I slipped my oar and made a strike at him
with the sprit. He dived, and so we chased him, hitting
and diving, diving and hitting, for some time, till we killed
him at last, and earned a good dinner. We pulled into
shore, took Shingle Short on board, and set out homeward
again, making a detour to the government schooner, which
was making very little way. We offered to take her in
tow, changed some of our oars, and soon left them out of
sight. In rounding the island we saw the *Water Witch*,
a beautiful cutter belonging to Captain Malcolm Smith of
Flinders, which had just come in. We arrived home

about dusk, and found Lucy Beadon, the Queen, just embarking for Badger. I was presented to her, and then went to tea, for which our long pull had made me quite ready. It may not seem very Sunday-like work, shooting geese and rabbits, but I must excuse myself by quoting my father's story of the Welsh parson whom the Bishop found fishing on a Sunday. " Dear me, Mr. Smith ! this is very wrong, fishing on a Sunday ; bad example, very." " Ah ! my Lord, but if your dinner was at the bottom of the river, you'd fish on a Sunday yourself." On Monday, the *Edward and Christopher* and the government schooner came in. I was pressed into the *Edward's* service, and found myself in a dingy, trying to pull her into harbour. I was hardly able to pull at all, as I had sprained my right wrist somehow the day before, and took the first opportunity I had of " skulking " the work. I had done enough, however, to make my wrist bad for some time. Amongst other things, the *Edward* brought Phillips' recall, for which I was very sorry, as I liked him much, and the loss of himself and party seriously decreased our already small population.

The *Edward* sailed on Thursday. A day or so after the *Boindie* left for Green Island, omitting to show her licence, and having the evident design of taking guano thence. The officer, as soon as he found this out, compelled a boat, that unluckily put in on her way from the Goose, to go after them and order them back—which they did ; Shingle Short being unusually absurd and frantic. All this time our lives were monotonous enough, only varied by visits from Queen Lucy and other islanders. I went to Badger on Sunday, September 7th, to pay a long talked-of visit to Lucy. Badger consists of plains and undulating hills, some bald, but for the most part more or less wooded. The views from the island are very much of the panoramic order ; Badger itself being very pretty and park-like. Some of the clumps of timber are both singular and graceful, consisting of she-oak, booby-aloe, and splendid mimosa (now in full bloom), a sort of pine something like a cypress or Oyster Bay pine—and many other shrubs, all mingled in picturesque confusion. We caught some Wallaby and kangaroo rats, in which the island abounds. One Wallaby, Jim Beadon caught alive ; it was taken possession of by Bluff (the skipper), with whom it soon became very tame. In the very centre of the island there are great masses of conglomerate—shells, sand, and clay, of such apparently recent formation, one is led to think that the sea has not very long receded therefrom. I used to think at one time that Tasmania had once been connected with Wilson's Promontory ; but I think otherwise now, and have little doubt that at some future age passengers may travel by rail from Hobart to Melbourne.

There is a beautiful and, to me, new kind of everlasting (*Nelectorium*) on this island, lilac and white coloured. On Mount Chappell we have them white and orange. There is a sort of wild tobacco (so called) growing in great profusion ; I brought some home to-day. Lucy Beadon tells me that it is a tolerable substitute, but hot ; I imagine, however, that if properly prepared, that fault might be remedied. Lucy entertained us very hospitably, amongst other eatables giving us cakes fried in (I think) mutton-bird oil, somewhat peculiar, but not nasty. We came home about dusk, after a very enjoyable day, and I taking Smith's ' Wealth of Nations ' from the " Royal " Library as a *pièce de résistance* for idle hours. I use it now as a narcotic, and find it equal to a hydra-headed sermon.

CAMP LIFE IN NEW ZEALAND.

———————

"I CAN'T make it out! I put that stick in this morning, and now it's nearly covered! There's been no rain these twenty-four hours, and the sun's been hot enough to skin a nigger; it must be the heat bringing all that snow down."

We were anxiously watching the river; it was between us and the stores, and till it was shallow enough to wade, there would be no hope of "tucker"—a bad look-out, as we were down to the last "split pea." On rushed the "Malakalaka," a fierce yellow torrent, marking the rapids in ever-changing whirls of foam, bearing with it huge helpless trees, freshly uprooted; now plunging swiftly on, now slowly circling in the eddies, then on again to bleach amid the dead forests, whose white bones strew the beaches and boulder banks of the West Coast.

The setting sun burnished the sombre pine-forests, flooded the beaches fringed with veronica and tuitui with yellow light, and turned to a fretwork of rose, silver, and gold, the distant fairy world of mountain and cloud. A glorious screen they seemed, hiding a greater glory beyond.

"How beautiful it is!" said I. "What would not some people give for scenery like this!"

"Scenery be hanged! scenery won't fill our bread-baskets," said Jack Robarts; "they're welcome to all my share for a beafsteak and a pot of porter."

"Don't forget the 'baccy,' Jack, in your bargain. But

there's waikas about ; let's bag a few before dark. If they're not beefsteak, they're satisfying at the price.

Wood-hens, or waikas, are a great stand-by in the bush. Their cry can be imitated, and a man knowing their language and character can catch them easily. They call each other by name, pronounced " Weeka," the latter syllable being shrill and prolonged, an octave higher than the first note. They have besides a ventri-loquial sound, a sort of grunt, which they use when alive, and their mates are with them ; after death it is the tone of voice in which they object to be plucked. The first time a dead waika argued the point with me I was com-pletely taken aback. I was alone, exploring in the neigh-bourhood of Lake Brunner, and was quietly plucking my bird for supper, when, hearing a grunt, I looked round everywhere for the bird I thought had come to supply me with a breakfast ; but no bird seemed to be near. Plucked again—again a grunt. Why, the bird's alive ! let us cut off his head and make sure. Plucked again : once more a grunt. I dropped it like a shot, and it was some minutes before I summoned courage to examine it. After a little time I found that, by compressing the breast, sounds could be produced at pleasure. I never came across any other kind of bird, to my knowledge, that was a ventriloquist. The woodhen is about the size of a common barn-door fowl ; its character is cunning, yet more fierce than cunning, and more inquisitive than either. Its fat forms a most penetrating oil for cleaning guns, &c.

Jack Robarts and I, provided with a stick and flat noose, went into a tolerably open scrub, and began chirping for robins. Very soon comes a robin, hopping with his head on one side, and a critical, doubtful sort of air, as much as to say, " That's not pure robin you're speaking, my fine fellow, but a very vile patois indeed." Swish ! goes my stick, and poor little robin will never be critical again ! Diggers never kill these little fellows wantonly, only as bait for eels and woodhens. In the bush, no matter where you pitch, the robin always comes and takes possession of you, and when any other of his tribe comes about, he bristles up his feathers, and fights for his crumbs and digger. Manfully he follows you to your work, on the look-out for worms, and when he gets any, instead of flying away and eating it up at once, he flies to the nearest tree, and sings at a great rate with the worm in his beak—a sort of grace before meat, no doubt. He is not at all pretty, like the Australian or European robin, but a little sober black and grey bird, with long legs, and a heavy paunch and big head ; like a Quaker, grave, but cheerful and spry withal, in good condition, but rather proppy about the legs. But here comes a " waika " cautiously stepping along, elevating and depres- sing the neck and head, in a manner peculiar to them. In a moment the dead robin flutters about at the end of a long stick between the waika and its prey. Waika walks round and round, pretending not to notice us, but eying us narrowly all the while. By-and-by a sort of grunt, I always keeping myself and trap temptingly in front of him, when all at once, caution forgotten, he dashes at the robin, alas ! to find himself dancing on nothing—condemned to be drawn and quartered for my supper. When Jack and I next met we found that our " poultry yard " had furnished us five birds for our entertainment ; so home, well-pleased, we went. We found our two mates there before us, also with some contributions to the family larder in the shape of a bird or two, some sow-thistles, the delicate young shoots of a charming little fern we used to call "asparagus." The fire was burning, and the last of our flour becoming "damper," the " billy " boiling ready for an infusion of the common " burr " or agrimony, a tolerable substitute for tea, not very much worse than the ordinary " post and rail " of the bush. It is a good anti-scorbutic, and to its occasional use, and a habit of eating every green weed that could be eaten, I attribute an immunity from scurvy, when other people about me have been suffering from it more or less.

It is time to introduce my mates. We were four in all, old diggers, ranging from twenty-five to thirty-five, rough and tough-looking bearded fellows, dressed in red shirt and trousers and belt with sheath knife ; in hats and boots we consulted our individual fancy, or necessity, as the case may be. Jack Roberts was a tall, handsome Englishman, the son of a Kent hopgrower ; he had held a commission in some cavalry regiment or other, but the pace being too fast for him, had to sell out and come to New Zealand to retrieve his fortunes. However, New Zealand finished what the crack regiment began, and he became a digger at the Watonuo, the first diggings worked in the Nelson province. Jack was possessed of the good-nature common to all very healthy men, and without being intellectual, had plenty of brains ; was a very good whist-player, a capital shot and moderate talker ; in his hours of ease a hard drinker ; at other times a hard and skilful worker, with a good nose for prospecting, and a sort of reputation for being a lucky man.

Tom Jenkins was a Welshman and a sailor, very superstitious, very vain, and very conceited, useful as an unconscious " butt " to while away a dull hour ; had a good ear for music, and a beautiful voice ; indeed he was a " dab " at shanty songs such as " Shenadore, I love your daughter." " Whiskey for my Johnny, oh ! " But, as he sang everything else in the same way, the effect was very ludicrous. For the rest, he was a good fellow enough, and he had a way of taking the pledge for the pure pleasure of breaking it. In his moments of remorse, which were not unfrequent, he became the victim of the most ingenious tortures we could devise.

Dick Dickson had been a good deal at sea, but for a

" digger " was well educated, very taciturn, yet popular. Of myself, the less said the better.

We were encamped on a little open shingle bed, surrounded and dotted with manuka in a pretty artificial kind of shrubbery ; for shelter we had a kind of miami of manuka boughs open at both ends, with a fly to keep out the rain. Our regular camp was about eight miles away, on the Buller reef. During a fortnight's stay, we had only once seen our claim, on account of the floods. The sandflies and mosquitoes there were simply intolerable, fairly driving us to our location, to be rid of them, while we waited the subsiding of the waters ; amusing ourselves with a self-acting cradle, washing the surface at our door, which, though very poor, paying eight or ten shillings per man a day, served to beguile the tedium of our enforced imprisonment, and to supply us with a little spree money. Meanwhile, we have played sad havoc with our woodhens, and divided our last smoke, with dark forebodings of a tobaccoless morrow.

Jack and Dickson are deep in the mysteries of " euker," playing for prospective nobblers ; our Welshman singing interminable and most doleful dittties ; while I, stretched on a bed of sweet springy manuka boughs, am lulled to that blessed sleep which comes alike to the just and the unjust after a day's toil in the New Zealand bush.

" I'm getting tired of fossicking about here," said Jack, next morning ; " it's all work and no play, it's only grog money at best. What are we to do to-day? the poultry here are getting rather scarce, and if we get ' grub,' let alone gold, we shall do very well. We're in a regular trap, that's certain."

" Gaff Bob [meaning me], it's plain there's a southerly wind in your baccy box. Look at him, sucking his pipe as though there were anything in it. Come, I'll give you half my dottle."

" I say, ' up, my ancient Briton ! ' you ought to be too hoarse to speak this morning. You made us all deaf last night with your caterwauling. Well, let's decide what we're going to do, and have it out with the savage Briton, and make him eat his leek after : it will save supper. I vote we go to Doughboy's Creek—there's some good nuggetty gold got there, and there may be many a crevice or two that old Doughboy has not rifled, though he ought to know the run of the place by this time."

" You can't do better," said Dickson ; " the patches are good, if you can get them ; besides, you are sure to get woodhens, and there used to be a garden ; there was one planted there, I know, when Antonio and Borneo Jack worked there." And so we agreed to take a turn up Doughboy's Creek, following a water-race which came thence and passed through our ground to a claim on the river Buller. We were soon on our road with our tools and our robins and snoozes, in search of gold and dinner, leaving Dickson behind (he had sprained his ankle), as cook, billy-washer, and chamber-maid.

" What do they call the creek and the men Doughboy, for ? " I asked, as we walked along to the jingling march-music of pick and tin dish.

" Why ! " answered Jack, " because he always eats his bread boiled instead of baked ; plaguey stick-jaw stuff it is too, a good meal of it makes one as stiff and helpless as a bottle."

" Well, but what sort of a chap is he ? "

" Oh, a regular rum old stick, a Swede or a German, I believe ; he mostly works a 'hatter.' He has worked with mates at times, and leaves them when the claim is done, and comes up a 'hatter' again. He's a regular old miser, never shouted in his life : he has lots of gold, they say, and never 'banks' it, but either keeps it about him, or plants it. For my part, I think planting a bad plan. I'd sooner spend it than take gold out of one place to put it in another, or under an old tree."

" It's a wonder," said I, " he never gets stuck up or murdered, living alone nearly always ! "

" Well, it's not so easy to make away with a man so well
known as he is. If the arms of the law were here, there
would be no trouble at all ; but Judge Lynch is different,
all eyes and arms like a spider. However, you'd better
try your hand—'faint heart '—you know the proverb. But
I wonder if old Doughboy's up here now ? "

" How should I know ? I hope so, for your sake, we'd
seize some baccy and flour too perhaps."

I was a little behind my mates, securing a refractory
woodhen, when I heard them calling me. They were
standing together looking intently, the Welshman as white
as milk. " What's up ? "

" There ! can't you see ? There's a dead man there, up
the bank, close to the wharee ! "

" Dead man ! nonsense ; he's dead drunk, more likely !"

" How the devil could he get drunk ? the creek does not
run brandy."

" Well, he must be asleep then. Here are his tools,
where he just left off work at that bit of a dam, and there
are his blankets airing. *He is dead !* By Jove ! there are
waikas at him. It's very odd, there are only ourselves and
Scottie here. Well ! let's go and have a look."

Neither of my mates would move a step, however ; had
the body been one of the ghosts Jenkins believed in, he
could not have shown more abject fear.

Robarts, so bold and fearless in most things, seemed to
have an unnatural horror of the uncanny sight. The
sight of a dead man in an utter solitude, yet with the
evidence of strength and work but recently suspended,
certainly gives one a kind of turn. Doughboy was lying
beside an old stump, with his face to the ground.

" By Jove, boys ! there's been foul play here," I said,
holding up first the broken stock of his gun that lay
beside him, and the barrel a yard or two off. " Look
here ; this looks like a struggle ! Come up, and help me
to look around."

Robarts, when he came up, began examining the broken stock. "It seems to me an odd break," said he ; "I wonder where the broken bit is." We could not find it.

"Don't you think that ten days of exposure to sun and rain " (for the man must have been dead about that time), "would make the fracture look old ? "

"Well, it might ; but do you think the poor devil's been murdered ? "

"Can't say ; it looks like it. But who could there be to murder him ? Scottie's party and ourselves are the only men on this side of the Buller, between the Malaka-laka and the Mornai, and they now have been up here ever so long."

"Well, it's passing strange ! But he may have fallen down in a fit, knocked against this stump, and tumbled his gun that way. Let's have a look at his wharre."

The wharre was only a few yards from where the body was lying. It was just such a place as a recluse might have built, with an idea of being tolerably comfortable. It was built of sawn timber, with some rude, but not in-effective efforts at ornamentation, and—wonder upon wonders !—floored with boards. Such a place was not to be found for miles and miles, except a government store some thirty miles off ; besides, all had just the appearance that a place occupied would have, the owner being only absent at work. We looked in his pockets to see if any-thing could be found by which we might possibly find out his real name, or give some clue to the mystery. We could not find any papers, and no treasure but one penny. While so searching, it suddenly struck us, that we might be suspected of the murder—if murder there had been—or, at least, of springing the plant. So, after considering the matter, we agreed that it would be better to leave things just as they were, till we could get Scottie to come up with us, who belonged to another party. His mates were away at the store, and prevented from returning by the flood, and he being nearly a stranger to us, could hardly be suspected of collusion.

From whatever cause, the death was very sudden, it was plain. His cradle had all the slides and green baize lining ready for washing; the tools were lying just where they had been used; the blankets had been hung out to air. "It must have been Scottie," I thought, but did not say so. My mates, whatever they thought, were equally reticent. Jenkins, indeed, either from superstition, fear, or consideration for his olfactory nerves, kept all through at a respectable distance. As we came up to him he said, "Why, you chaps are smoking!"

"Yes," I said, handing him a stick of negro-head; "you'd better have a draw or two."

"Where did you get it?"

"From our friend Doughboy, up there."

"Then I'll smoke manuka bark first. Ough! you pip! smoking a dead man's tobacco! and what's that you're carrying?"

"Flour, to be sure."

"Well, I'll starve before I eat any of it."

"Very happy to hear you say so. You'll make a lovely corpse, and be buried with all the honours due to an ancient Briton and descendant of Caractacus."

I must confess, however, that we left our dead waikas, and released one we had alive, as it seemed to us we should be but cannibals to have eaten their *confrères* revelling on our dead brother ont he hill-side. I know I mentally vowed not to eat one caught within a mile of the place—a poor look-out, but for my smuggled flour.

As soon as we got home, after telling Dickson the story, Edwards and I went to see Scottie, an honest, but withal shrewd Scotchman, with light hair, and all-round whiskers and beard framing a stout pleasant face. He promised to meet us next morning, and, on hearing our dilemma about the man-eating poultry, shot us some pigeons to take home. The pigeon here is a very beautiful bird as to plumage and shape, but has a lumbering flight, and is exceedingly stupid. They are easily killed in the low scrub with a spear, or snared with a long thin stick, with a noose at the end. All you have to do is to push your stick through the boughs, till your flax noose is close to its beak ; the booby stretches its neck to see what's up, and goes to pot or spit accordingly. However, the pigeons proved a very welcome addition to our supper, though they are somewhat dry and insipid ; and I grieve to say that hunger so far overcame the noble Jenkins that, after a great many virtuous reflections, he pitched into Doughboy's scones and tobacco in a way that would have been a caution to less squeamish critics than we were. In the remorse that followed, he entranced us with the mad yarns of "corpse lights," and other "devices of the devil," that flourish to this day in the "land of the leek."

Next day we went up with Scottie, and made a strict search for Doughboy's plant, or papers, in every place we could think of, likely or unlikely ; but without result. The worst business of all was searching the pockets of the clothes he wore, Scottie holding them open with a long-handled shovel, I at work rifling them, with my hand wrapt in one piece of baize, and my nose in another. I only found a powder-flask and some odds and ends.

"Thank God ! that job's done with ! What shall we do with the body ? Leave it ! He'll be as well here as anywhere else."

" Nay, give the puir fellow Christian burial."

" Very well, put him in the blankets ; there's a great heap of dry wood—we can burn him."

This proposal shocked Scottie, who explained that he did not call that Christian burial, and should feel very

uncomfortable if we did not give him a grave of some
sort ; then, too, if the bones were ever wanted for exami-
nation, we should know where to find them.

"The deuce ! " I thought ; "does the man suspect us,
I wonder?" So I did not argue the point ; though a
burial is enough to make a man dread to die, in its utter
loathsomeness. " *Death* leaves only the beautiful," says
Hood ; but *burial* all that is foul and hideous. How
any man can consign those he loves to corruption, instead
of yielding them to bright beautiful fire, at once the
purifier, destroyer, and preserver, is past my under-
standing.

We laid his winding-blankets underneath, and rolled
him into them with our long-handled shovel; however,
he left his head behind him—so much violence must have
been used ere he died. At last we laid what we picked
up of him in one of his old prospecting shafts. Poor
fellow ! he little thought when toiling, sinking it, that it
would prove his grave.

On the way home we hazarded many conjectures as to
the cause of death. Scottie, however, was silent, not
offering a single opinion of any kind. He borrowed a
book from us in the evening, as he said he felt "lonely
like," and as though he carried a photograph of the day's
scene with him. The book nearly proved his death,
which, being unpleasant for him, would have been decidedly awkward for us. When we went to his place in
the morning, we found it burnt down, and himself minus
hair, eyebrows, and whiskers.

It appears he fell asleep while reading the book we had
lent him, and awoke to find the place in a blaze. He
hardly knew how he managed to get as clear as he did.
Not the strangest part of the business was, that he had
put the powder-flask under his head, and though the place
was quite consumed, it never went off. Had it done so,
and he had been blown up, everybody would have believed

that we had murdered Doughboy, and put Scottie out of the way to keep him silent.

In the afternoon some men came over the " Buller," and took Scottie and ourselves to the stores, where I at last got the clue to the mystery we were so puzzled about, and which Scottie held. The stores were situated at the juncture of the " Buller," and the combined waters, boiling through a narrow chasm in the rocks, which was crossed by a bridge, in the shape of two spars, one to step on, the other to give some sort of hand-hold. It was not a very pleasant place to cross, as the waters, circling, twisting, and writhing in its narrow walls. were very apt to make one giddy; and once fall in, there would be little chance of rising again.

These rapids are not uncommon in New Zealand rivers : they are always beautiful, and sometimes terrible in their grandeur. There were a few tents at the Mangles, occupied by people who had taken up abandoned claims, just to earn " tucker " or make a bit of a rise, while looking about for a better claim. The stores, three in number, were of a mixed order of architecture—" stabs and cant up." The goods were packed up to them on bullocks and horses from " depôts " about twenty or thirty miles off ; all the stores were " grog shanties " as well, and were often scenes of rude dissipation, though, owing probably to the absence of the gentler sex, who, however peaceable in themselves, are fertile in wars for others, rows seldom occurred of more consequence than a civil growl among mates, or a fight over a game of cards. It was no uncommon thing for a mob of men to drink the stores dry, though the Buller was turned on the grog casks pretty liberally, and the devices for procuring the semblance of grog to prolong the " spree " were amusing. On one occasion an inventive genius took a " nobbler " of " pain killer " pronounced it good, and the whole stock was sold

T

at a shilling a nip, much to the profit of the vendors, and without harm to the consumers.

We found a great many people there on our arrival. Besides diggers in the neighbourhood, there were people on their way up from town; some to the "manner born" who were swallowing the most marvellous stories wholesale, and drinking whatever was offered them, till they became thoroughly bewildered. Others were old hands, who had made their piles, but fallen among thieves or sirens in Nelson, and come back penniless. Others again, with heavy little bags, were on their way to lighten them in Christmas festivities in town, or to gladden their families (if they had any) with a sight of themselves and their gold.

Of course, on our arrival, we told our story about Doughboy, and the general belief (which I myself had come to), was that he had died in a fit. Some few who were strangers to us thought otherwise, but did not say so, and the affair was soon forgotten in the general bustle.

Two of the storekeepers challenged any of the diggers to a game at "whist," which was immediately taken up by Edwards and myself. It was under difficulties, however; the uproar of Babel was a fool to the confusion of tongues around us. On bags of flour, on tea-chests at the "bar," games of "euchre," "cribbage" and "all fours," &c., were going on simultaneously; all the interjections peculiar to the games in many languages, interlarded with a profusion of strange oaths.

Jenkins and another were singing for a wager. His opponent had just roared "Still so gently o'er me stealing," with a voice like the bull of "Bashan;" Jenkins was hard at it chanting "Willy O'Reilly;" the style of his singing had touched a sympathetic chord in the breast of a drunken new chum (a runaway sailor), who came in with tunes of other songs by way of accompaniment; while a "Lyall's Creeker," not to be out of the general harmony, sang his "National Anthem :"—

" From Ballarat to Bendigo
    Turn to Tuapeka,
There's not a boy for work or spree
    Can lick your Lyall's Creeker,
We pick the pockets of the State,
    And spend the 'loot' together,
We blast the rocks and dam the creek
    And doubly damn the weather."

To crown all, a " broth of a boy from the Emerald Isle "
was dancing a "double shuffle" on the counter, to
Garryowen, played by his mate on a broken-winded
accordion.   Our whist soon made way for *vingt-et-un*, and
that in its turn for euchre, till it was time for a bath and
breakfast ; sleep of course was out of the question, except
to a few by a " sleepy Bacchus."

After breakfast, I saw Scottie and one of his mates, and
Jack Robarts beckoning to me.   " Hi! Scottie has something to say to you about Doughboy.   He was murdered
after all."

" Yes," said Scottie, " I was up there the day he died,
and this was the way of it.   Three men came to our place
and asked us if we could put them over the " Buller " in our
canoe, as they were going " Lyall's Creek way."   We said
yes, and they replied ' All right,' they would be back in the
evening.   They were camped where you were.   Now one of
these was named Bill—did you know him ? " " Well, I've
seen him, I think ; a red-haired man, has a bit of a farm
down Partridge Valley way."

" That's him ; and it was he that killed old Doughboy."

" The devil he did ! "

" Yes; it so happened that day there was something
wrong with our race; the water was very slack, and we
thought the mouth of the race (just where Doughboy
worked, you know) was stopped up or something ; so
Paddy and I went up to see.   On our way up we met
Bill's mates coming down the race; asked us if we had

T 2

seen Bill. ' No ?' ' Oh, then he must be out shooting.' Well, when Paddy and I got to the creek, old Doughboy was at work at that bit of dam, just where we saw his tools lying, his blankets out to air, cradle ready, and everything, except himself and his gun, exactly as when you found them. We did what was wanting to our race in no time. Had a smoke and a yarn with Doughboy, and started home again. As we went down, met Bill, who asked us if Doughboy was at home? and if there were any pigeons about? When we got to your camp, we heard a shot or two, but of course thought nothing of it, and went home. In the evening down came Bill's two mates, but no Bill. ' Where's your mate '? we asked. ' Oh ! he's gone across the Malakalaka to get a few more stores, and will join us at the other side to-morrow. He'll easily catch us up ; we have tidy heavy swags, he'll be middling light. Well, my gentleman did cross the Malakalaka, but got away like a ' red shank,' Nelson way. He went to Coleman's stores, right enough, but would not stop the night—affected he wanted to catch his mates up ; but he went to town, for two or three of these chaps saw him."

" Do you think his mates were in it ? "

" No ! for they were evidently waiting for him. I saw their fire near the ' Martin ' all day."

" Why did you not tell us all this before, Scottie ? "

" Well, because you were strangers to me; and as for that Jenkins of yours, you had better say nothing to him now ! "

" If he was murdered, no doubt this Bill must have done it ; but do you know I suspected you, Scottie."

" So did I, till you buried him," said Robarts.

" Well, I thought you would," said Scottie, " for he could not have died in a fit."

" Why not ? "

" Well, a fit, to smash him up as he was, must have been convulsive, whereas his attitude was perfect rest, his head on his arm, as if asleep. Depend upon it, he was put in that position."

After some further conversation we agreed to state all these matters on paper, and forward a memorandum to Government. This we did, and took it over to Coleman, the storekeeper, to forward it, as we were alike innocent of post-offices, policemen, and parsons.

When Coleman read the document he would have nothing to do with it ; said Bill was a most respectable man ; would not hurt a fly ; good-natured, had helped him to build his store when pressed, and wouldn't take a penny for it, and so on. The end of it was we burned our memo, concluding it was no business of ours, and that we might only make enemies and do no good.

Some two months after these events I happened to walk over land from Nelson to Christchurch, having missed the steamer, and went some three or four miles out of my way to pay a few shillings I owed an hotel-keeper when I had been laid up in his house with a badly sprained ankle. He was a professional man of considerable versatility,—" Davenport Brothers," " Professor Parker," and " Farquharson " in one. " I hear old Doughboy's dead," he said. " I miss him ; he used to come up here once or twice a year for a quiet spree." I then told him the whole story, and our suspicions of Bill, who was a near neighbour of his. " Indeed you are right, he came in here just about that time, one night, as I was closing ; he seemed excited and tired. ' Hullo!' I said ' you've not been long on the diggins this time.' ' No,' says he ; ' by the Powers I've touched lucky at last, old fellow: look here ! ' and he put a tidy bag into my hand, and what struck me at once was, that it was tied with a peculiar knot that I never saw anyone use but Doughboy; you know, from old habit, I can't help noticing those things. When he saw me eyeing the bag so closely, he snatched it out of my hand, drank off his grog, and I have never seen him again. He went next steamer under a feigned name, and bagged a lot of money my son-in-law gave him to bank for him. It looked suspicious then, but now it's plain he was the murderer."

Now this is a true story, an incident out of my life when exploring in New Zealand many years ago (1862). I have never met any of the persons mentioned in it since, but I feel sure that wherever the man I have called Bill is, he will have a light gold bag and a heavy heart.

LONDON: PRINTED BY EDWARD STANFORD, 55, CHARING CROSS, S.W.

www.ingramcontent.com/pod-product-compliance
Lightning Source LLC
Chambersburg PA
CBHW030622030726
47497CB00006B/1605